I0618657

Sherlock Holmes

Gray Manor

By

G. L. Schulze

Sherlock Homes – Gray Manor

Copyright@2017 by G.L. Schulze – All rights reserved

No part of this publication may be reproduced, stored in a retrieval system or transmitted in any way by any means, electronic, mechanical, photocopy, recording or otherwise without the permission of the author except as provided by USA copyright law.

This novel is a work of fiction. Names, characters, locations, descriptions, entities, and incidents included in the story are products of the author's imagination. Any resemblance to actual persons, events, and entities is entirely coincidental.

Published by GLS Press

Cover design support by Holli Chlebowski – Graphic Designer

Book design copyright @ Holli Chlebowski

Cover photo design by G. L. Schulze

Published in the United States of America

ISBN: 13: 978-0692877937

ISBN: 10: 0692877932

Fiction/ General/Action Adventure/Mystery

Other Books by G. L. Schulze

The Young Detectives' Mystery Series:

The Secret Treasure of Pirate's Cove – Book One

The Top Secret Secret of Teddy Rigetta – Book Two

The Hidden Secret of Towering Pines Manor – Book Three

The Secret of the Sacred Mountain – Book Four

The Secret at the Bottom of Emerson's Cove – Book Five

Sherlock Holmes

Gray Manor

Chapter One

"Dorthea? Dorthea Pearl? Is that really you?" Watson called out.

The woman approaching from the opposite direction stopped abruptly. Her mind had been on another matter entirely and the calling of her name startled her. Panic gripped her, her heart raced and her breath caught in her throat. Color drained from her already pale face. Frightened, she looked about in every direction until she identified the man who had stopped several feet before her.

"John? Oh my goodness!" she cried with obvious relief. "It is you!" She rushed to him and embraced him to her. "Why John Watson, I hardly recognized you!"

"And I you," Watson exclaimed, returning the embrace. "I am sorry if my outburst frightened you but seeing you here is such a wonderful surprise. It has been years since we have seen each other. I believe the last time was…."

"Was when Ambrose died. It's all right to say it. It has been many years now and I am able to speak of it without too much pain."

"Yes, I am very sorry about Ambrose. He was a dear friend and I was very much grieved at his death. But, enough of the past. What brings you to London? St. Stephens is quite a distance."

"Yes, it is," Dorthea hesitated. She searched Watson's eager face and wondered; should she tell him or

1

not? St. Stephens was many years ago and John had been a close friend, a trusted friend. But those years were so long ago, and the tragedy with Ambrose she did not wish to relive in light of her current situation. She remained undecided. "Yes, it is some distance, but I was rather looking forward to the trip. The trains now are swift and very accommodating."

"And when did you arrive?" Watson asked. He was still clasping her hands and sheepishly released them, taking note of her somber attire.

"Let's walk, John. I must return." Dorthea Pearl linked her arm in his. "There is still much to do. I arrived several weeks ago. My second cousin on my mother's side, you remember Agnes? Agnes Tidwell? She wrote me some time ago saying she was not well and would very much like to see me. There was such a yearning, a sadness, in her letter, that I came to London at the first opportunity."

"Your Cousin Agnes is here in London?" Watson asked. "I did not know."

"Yes. After Winston and I married, she was alone once more. Due to her advancing years, she decided to sell her small cottage and move here to London to be nearer to her remaining relatives. I have missed her greatly. She is….was… very dear to me and I should have visited more often, but I was so caught up in my own affairs. I regret that now, John.

"She wrote, imploring me to come and I arrived nearly too late. Cousin Agnes was gravely ill and passed shortly after my arrival. It's been an utterly treacherous ordeal, I know, especially since I am still troubled by my own turmoil. But, she was my last remaining relative, and I am happy that I came. She was so much more to me than a cousin, as you know, and she drew much comfort from my presence. Her passing was peaceful."

"I am sorry about Cousin Agnes. Please accept my condolences. But about this other matter you just mentioned, your own turmoil? Dorthea, you must tell me all about it. Perhaps I can be of some help. I owe you that much. I have been so remiss in …."

"Don't be silly, John. You owe me nothing and furthermore, I do not know if you can help. My turmoil is great and frankly I am somewhat ashamed to speak of it." Dorthea stopped abruptly on the walk and turned to Dr. Watson. Tears threatened her dark brown eyes and he quickly reached for his handkerchief. "Oh, John!"

"My dear, Dorthea! What is it? I insist you allow me to help you….no wait. I do not know whether you are aware, but I have taken up residence with Sherlock Holmes. We began as borders sharing lodgings and expenses only, but over the years have grown to be quite good friends. Holmes calls himself a consulting detective and has worked numerous cases solving problems of everyday persons such as yourself. He is very good; the best. Besting the police more times than not. Please, please. You must come with me and explain your situation to the both of us and I am most confident he will be able to assist you no matter what it is."

"I could not bother…."

"It is no bother, my dear friend. Allow me to escort you back to your cousin's home, then I will return home and inform Holmes that you will be paying us a visit, let's say, this afternoon? Two o'clock? I will not take no, Dorthea."

Dorthea looked into the face of her dear friend, the look of concern evident upon his furrowed brow, the look of determination set in his eyes. A weary but grateful smile touched her lips and she blinked away the tears. She put her head to Watson's shoulder and sighed. She was tired. Oh so very tired. Managing alone with everything the past few months was taking its toll upon her not only in her mind but also her body. There were days she felt she could not go on. Perhaps this chance encounter with her old friend, John Watson, was meant to be. Perhaps John and this Sherlock Holmes really could help her make some sense of what was happening to her. Explain away the madness that haunted her every waking moment. Her heart lifted and for one fleeting moment she felt hope. "If you insist, John, how can I possibly refuse. Perhaps there is something that can be done. Two o'clock. Come. Cousin Agnes' home is not far. I am very happy that I have seen you once more."

Watson quickened his pace towards 221B Baker Street, his mind reeling with concern for his friend. He thought back over his conversation with Dorthea Pearl. What did she mean, no one could help her? And what did she mean by Cousin Agnes being her last surviving relative? What of Winston and her child? Just what exactly was going on at St. Stephens that had his good friend in such a wretched state? He chastised himself for allowing her to convince him that she would arrive on her own. He should have insisted that he make arrangements for her travel. But it was too late for that now. The thing to do now was to prepare Sherlock Holmes for a new case.

The mention of it was barely out of his mouth before Holmes threw down the paper he was reading, bolted upright in the chair and shouted, "What? You have promised her that I would help? How could you make such a commitment on my behalf, Watson? You are not aware of my other obligations and…."

"Oh for goodness sake, Holmes! You have been sitting in that chair smoking up the place for nearly three days now. Do not tell me of your other obligations. You have none other than the mariner case and that is near complete. Dorthea Pearl is an old and dear friend. There is something wrong. She needs our help, Holmes."

"Well, she is your friend. You help her."

"I do not understand your contentious attitude today, Holmes. You are in such a foul mood. What you need is a case and this case you shall take. I will have no more of your insolence! Mrs. Pearl will be arriving at two. Be here. Be ready!" Watson shouted. Red faced and fuming, he turned on his heels and slammed the door to his private quarters behind him. He leaned against the door, forcing himself to breathe slowly, to calm his anger. Of all the times for Holmes to ….ahh, but then that was the way of Holmes wasn't it? Putting forth a charade of disinterest when coursing through his veins was a blood boiling and eager to begin.

He walked to the window and stared at the street below. He had walked the distance from Cousin Agnes' home to 221B Baker Street, the thought of something, anything, plaguing Dorthea Pearl tearing at his heart. He'd known her years before, a sweet and charming woman whose friendship towards him had not faltered despite the outcome of that summer's celebration all those years ago.

His mind ran rampant with what could be affecting his friend until he had talked himself into an agitated state concerning her safety. By the time he'd reached Baker Street he was already on edge. When confronted with

Holmes' argumentative and hostile attitude, he'd played the fool and jumped headlong into Holmes' trap.

At the slamming of Watson's door, Holmes smiled and nodded. He knew the instant that Watson walked through the door of their apartments that something was on his mind. The edgy manner was evident when Watson entered and flung off his hat and overcoat; the wringing of his hands as he spoke and paced the room; the anxious concern in the manner of his speech. Not only were these signs of an issue of immediate concern, but were characteristic signs of a personal involvement.

He really did have nothing to do. No cases, no obligations. He'd sunk into a lethargic slump of moping about the apartment, smoking scads of tobacco and not even bothering to dress from his morning clothes for days. Not only did Dorthea Pearl interest him as a possible client, her relationship to John Watson piqued his curiosity even more. Obviously somewhere in Watson's background there lurked deeply hidden secrets from his past. Else why his indignant attitude over Holmes' provocation? He decided to dress.

Promptly at two, Dorthea Pearl arrived. She hesitated outside the freshly painted door of 221B Baker Street and wondered if she were making the right decision in keeping her appointment with John and his friend, Sherlock Holmes. Should she tell them? Should she tell them everything? She was torn between not wishing to burden others with her problems, yet the need was overwhelming to pour out her burden in the hope of gaining some sense of sanity back. She was torn between the desire for someone to help her yet wishing it not be John Watson, for once the burden was unleashed, he would see the inner madness of her soul. She hesitated, her hand poised in the air. She decided the thought of John recoiling away from her once he knew the truth was more tolerable to bear than completely losing the remainder of her sanity. She rang the bell.

Watson paced his private quarters for nearly an hour, anger still burning from Holmes' foul mood, before descending into the study where the now dressed Holmes sat in his usual chair, a newspaper in hand.. He quickly ordered fresh tea and raspberry tarts, the pot steaming on the table, the tarts still warm. Watson cast Holmes a look of smoldering irritation on his way to the window and watched as the cab pulled away. It wasn't long before two sets of footsteps sounded on the stairs. In a moment Mrs. Hudson opened the door and escorted the woman in.

Holmes rose to meet her. He took in her appearance and saw nothing extraordinary about the woman that entered. Normal height, not much more than five feet three. Shapely, well rounded and full busted, a child perhaps. Yet her face held a haunted look of sadness, one that slowly overwhelms the physical attributes until beauty becomes plain. Her clothes were simple, yet elegant, the black satin gown single folded to the floor with a matching bonnet tied neatly to her head. The color of grief. Soft brown tendrils curled from the bonnet and as she began to remove it, Holmes noticed the premature hint of gray along the temples. Her face was lovely but the dark brown eyes beneath arched brows were shadowed with an inner depth of sadness. Dark circles were unmistakable and her forced smile did nothing to hide her apprehension.

"Hello, John. And you must be Sherlock Holmes?" Dorthea smiled in Watson's direction, then stretched her hand to Holmes. "John has told me so much about you.

He speaks very highly of you as an investigating detective and believes that you will most certainly be able to help me with my situation."

Holmes raised his eyebrows ever so slightly at the compliment and despite the click of his heel and a quick bow to Dorthea Pearl, could not hide the obvious pleasure of it. "Mrs. Pearl, Watson has said not much of you I am afraid. But I believe he wished me to draw my own conclusions without prejudice. Sit, please. Watson, if you would pour the tea? It is fresh, Mrs. Pearl and our housekeeper, Mrs. Hudson, is noted for her raspberry tarts. Please help yourself. I find a hot tea and something palatable to be a calming and soothing remedy for one who has much to tell."

"Thank you so much, Mr. Holmes." Dorthea placed her bonnet very purposefully with the gloves and her handbag on the table. Sitting in the chair indicated, she accepted her tea, sipped once of the steaming beverage then placed it carefully on the table at her side. The bite on the raspberry tart was barely a nibble before it, too, was set back to the plate on the table.

Holmes resumed his position, sitting in the arm chair near the fireplace and Watson pushed aside the pillows on the sofa and sat down. He looked from Holmes to Dorthea and back again but could not discern any thought Holmes may be having. An eerie silence of anticipation filled the room. The three sat quiet, the stillness marred only by the ticking of the mantle clock. With a heavy sigh and a weary smile, Dorthea looked about the room, dragging her gaze from item to item, reluctant to begin, not knowing where to begin, not knowing how to begin, until at last, no longer able to avoid the intense stare of the grey blue eyes of Sherlock Holmes, her gaze lighted upon him. With an apologetic smile, she said, "I do not know where to begin, to tell you the truth."

"Why not at the beginning. Watson here knows everything about you. I know none at all. Start at the beginning."

"Very well. My mother died when I was five and I can honestly say I do not remember much of her except that she was a tall woman with yellow hair who smiled and sang to me. My father was a minister. When my mother died, we moved many times and after that, memories of my mother began to blur more and more as the moves took us away from familiar territory."

Holmes sighed inwardly. That beginning was not what he had in mind, but as Dorthea Pearl was *that* close of a friend to Watson, he decided to allow her to continue. He leaned casually back into the chair taking note of her hands now clasped so tightly in her lap, the knuckles shown white.

"I had an older brother, Ambrose, who despite being nearly ten years my senior, was very fond of me. We were not merely siblings, Mr. Holmes, we were best friends, especially after the death of our mother. Father became quiet and morose and I noticed a terrible sadness about him. He spent more time in the church begging God's forgiveness for his sins than he ever spent with Ambrose and me. I often wondered what was so terrible that my father had done that he should have to beg forgiveness for, but it was only later, when I grew into adulthood, that I came to see that my father blamed himself for my mother's death. For years it tore him up inside and one day, God answered his prayers and he was taken also. I was relieved for his sake for I truly believe him to be with my mother and he must surely be happy now.

"Upon his death when I was twelve, I was taken to live with my cousin Agnes, who at that time resided in St. Stephens. Ambrose was already a grown man and had joined in military service. I do not know if you are familiar with the area?" Holmes shook his head. "No? St. Stephens is a small town off the mainland on the westernmost coast of England. It is an old mining town of tin and copper and at one time was a large supplier of that product. Several years ago it reached its peak in production and the mines began to falter. For many years now, the mines have been closed and many of the people have gone. There was no work you see and people had to leave the area to find work in order to survive.

"I enjoyed living with Cousin Agnes and although there were very few children left to draw friendship with, I did enjoy walking the cliffs that overlooked the ocean, and scouring the old caves left behind by the mines. It was there, when I was but seventeen, that I met and fell in love with Winston Pearl." Dorthea closed her eyes for a fleeting moment and thought of those happy days with Winston at St. Stephens. The soft sea breeze, the soaring of gulls overhead, the touch of Winston's hand in hers as they strolled along the beaches.

"It was a wonderful summer, Mr. Holmes," she sighed and continued at last. "And Winston and I fell madly in love. I know most people would not understand how such a bond could form so quickly, but within three months, Winston asked me to marry him. He was everything I had ever dreamed of, tall and handsome, kind and gentle. He had a way of talking to people that made them feel important no matter their station in life. Of course I consented.

"Winston was an engineer at the Botallara Mine and he was very good at his chosen profession. There were, however, setbacks when the owners wanted him to have the men extend the underground tunnels beneath the beach. He refused at first stating they were already too dangerously far out beneath the sea and the passing of the tide each evening was eroding the integrity of the earth above the tunnels. He no sooner spoke those words when there was a massive collapse of a tunnel and three of the miners lost their lives.

"Winston was devastated. He took the blame of course, saying he should have spoken sooner. But it was not his fault, Mr. Holmes. He was under the employ of the Botallara Mine owners and despite misgivings, had to carry out orders. He feared for his job you see because we had just found out that I was with child. He wanted to be sure he could be a good provider.

"It was about that time that Winston received an urgent message from his father to return home. And that was the same time that my brother Ambrose…well….he died." Dorthea cast Watson a furtive look and Watson immediately averted his gaze, looking from the wall to the floor, his face flushed. Holmes noted Watson's discomfort, his abrupt aversive reaction and wondered at the circumstances of Ambrose's death.

"Go on Mrs. Pearl. Then what happened," he urged.

"It was also at that time that Winston was forced to explain to me of his heritage." Dorthea stopped and took in a deep breath. She sipped once more of the tea and despite her every effort, tears rose in her eyes and she put her head down.

Putting aside his shamed discomfort Watson rose and said, "Would you like more tea?"

"Yes, thank you, John. These raspberry tarts are really very tasty. I should get the recipe and have Justine, my cook, try them," Dorthea smiled, blinking away the tears, grateful that no more was mentioned regarding Ambrose.

"And what exactly was Winston's heritage, Mrs. Pearl?" Holmes asked. Watson refilled the tea cups and returned to the sofa.

"Winston had never spoken of his past or his family and, quite frankly, I simply never asked. He told me he was the only heir to Gray Manor, a very wealthy landholding to the eastern coast of England. He and his father had had a falling out over his choice of occupation years earlier and his father had disowned him. But once he received information that Winston had married and was now expecting a child, he had decided to make amends with Winston and now called him back to the family estate."

"Pardon me, but how did his father come to know that?" Holmes asked.

"I do not know, but I knew by the manner in which Winston explained to me of his father that he still held ill feelings, but he would not tell me why. He did say that despite the fact that he and his father were not close there was no reason why I should not make up my own mind about the man. Perhaps things would be different. At least in that regard Winston was willing to keep his pride in check."

"So you went to Gray Manor?" Holmes asked.

"Yes. It is situated in Cornwall near a small village called Cadwith. Winston's father, James Pearl, came into possession of Gray Manor when his wife, Anna Eleanore Gray Pearl, died. She was the only daughter of the late

Lord Farley Bartholomew Gray, the only living relative actually, and so inherited the property upon her marriage to James Pearl despite the laws that women could not hold title back then. They…he…Lord Farley Gray owned the entire county, the small village, the people, the fishing rights, the cove, the coastline, the surrounding area…well for miles. He was a brutal and selfish man, according to Winston and treated those about him as less than servants, expecting their loyalty and their tithing whether they could afford it or not. It appeared that the son-in-law, James Pearl, Winston's father, was his equal in that regard and that Winston and he argued over this many times. That was one of the reasons why Winston left and never mentioned him to me."

"Until it became a matter of necessity," Holmes remarked.

"Yes, until it became a matter of necessity."

"And what was the reason for Lady Anna Pearl's death? Did Winston ever say?"

"No, Mr. Holmes, I was led to understand that she died during childbirth and he never knew his mother for he never spoke of her."

"And despite all of this, you still went to Gray Manor?" Watson asked.

"Yes. I felt there was something that Winston was not telling me and I thought the only way I was going to find the truth was to go there and actually see for myself. It was I who insisted we return to Gray Manor. Expecting a child changes one's perspective of parenthood and I thought it best for Winston and his father to come to terms with their differences and perhaps rekindle their relationship. I thought to my love and friendship with Ambrose and had high hopes for them both. And after the incident at the mine, Winston reluctantly decided it was time to go."

"And so you went," Holmes remarked.

"Yes. And so we went. I can still remember that first drive through the tiny village of Cadwith. It is primarily a fishing village but there are a few farms in the outlying areas. There is a narrow road that runs through the town then travels for several miles through a heavily forested area before it rises sharply. Then it levels onto the fields of the farmers there. Once we reached the top of the rise, well, my breath was taken aback. There before me was the most beautiful manor house I had ever seen. I do not know much of architecture, Mr. Holmes, but the place was grand. Approaching from the front there are three distinct wings to the house. The center being the entrance hall with a left wing and right wing that meets in the center of each floor as it rises. There are more rooms than anyone could possibly count. Yet, even as I was completely entranced by the sheer grandness of the thing, something deep inside of me was frightened for it had an aura of danger, of impending doom as though there was something sinister about it."

Holmes detected the slight tremble in Dorthea Pearl's voice and was intrigued by her choice of words. His eyebrows arched. "Sinister?"

"Perhaps sinister is too harsh a word, Mr. Holmes. But when the carriage drew to a stop on the hill, a cold shiver ran down my spine and a foreboding of evil overwhelmed my entire being. Winston simply thought I was cold and I could not explain to him my fear. We approached the house which had been built upon a rising knoll. It stood at its summit, stark and bare; all manner of trees had been cut back away from the house on the three sides as though there was a fear.....” Dorthea shook her head.

“We drew closer and I saw that my original impression of grandeur was misled for the grounds had not been kept for quite some time. The stone wall was in complete shambles with stones fallen everywhere. Grass grew tall and uncut throughout. Shrubs had been allowed to grow wild and misshapen and I knew by Winston’s posture that he already regretted his decision to bring me there.”

“Why didn’t you simply leave?” Watson asked.

“We had come all that way, John. Despite Winston’s misgivings, we had to at least try.”

“I see. Please go on, Mrs. Pearl.” Holmes made it plain to Watson not to interrupt further by a simple rising of his eyebrows.

“There were no servants to greet us and that upset Winston much more than the neglected state of the estate. The driver of the carriage we hired let us off and quickly turned and departed and I thought he, too, could sense the danger there. We entered the house alone and found it to be dark and unclean, a foul smell, a musty smell of old dust and decay permeated the air. It reminded me of entering a tomb. Once again, a chill went through me but before I could say anything an elderly man came forth from out of one of the darkened rooms. He explained that he was Jessop, the only male servant left still attending to Lord Pearl and that his wife Elizabeth was the cook. The entire place was dark and cold and the grandeur that once possessed the place had been replaced and filled with sadness, darkness and shadows. It clearly had been as neglected as the exterior and I felt an overwhelming sadness for Winston to have had to return home under those conditions.

"Jessop carried a lighted candle and led us upstairs to the library where he said Lord Pearl spent most of his waking hours. The door there was ajar. As we walked down the hall towards the room, our shadows danced grotesquely on the walls around us and another shiver ran through me. I could feel the fear growing inside of me, fear for the baby I carried inside of me. The air grew heavy and it was difficult to breath and I wanted to turn and run. I can honestly tell you, Mr. Holmes, that if I had not been holding Winston's hand I would have certainly done just that. In retrospect, it is what I should have most certainly done. But it was his turn for reassurances and he squeezed my hand and smiled at me and together we entered the library." Dorthea shivered involuntarily at the thought.

"Are you all right, Dorthea?" Watson asked.

"I…I'm fine, John, thank you."

"You were entering the library, Mrs. Pearl." Once more Holmes cast a look of irritation at Watson.

"Yes, the library. The library was no different than that from which we had come. It was dark and cold and so much more oppressive because of the shelves and books. Even in the meager thread of light from the candles on the desk I could see the place was covered with a thick layer of dust and hanging cobwebs. It seemed to me there were shadows in every corner, eyes watching us, an evil that lurked throughout the house but lived in that library.

"And then we saw him. A thin man, shrunken with age and illness, sitting in the chair at the desk, hunched over the papers there. Lord James Pearl rose from where he had been sitting and simply stared at Winston. There was no greeting, no welcoming manner about him in the least. He then turned to me and said, 'So this is the woman? And you are with child? Good. Perhaps there may yet be a Pearl deserving of my holdings. Jessop see to them' and with that he walked away."

"Quite strange, to say the least," Watson said. "Apparently he had no intention of mending the rift between himself and your husband, Dorthea."

"No, I thought the same thing myself, and I instantly regretted my insistence to Winston that we come to the manor for that purpose."

"Despite this, you and your husband stayed at Gray Manor?" Holmes asked.

"I am afraid we were forced to, Mr. Holmes. I became seriously ill soon after our arrival and the doctor was sent for. Because of my baby, you see, I was laid to bed until delivery. Several months passed and with each passing day I could see Winston change. He no longer smiled or hummed when he worked. His pallor turned ashen and he looked like he was not eating very well. His sleep was troubled and many times during the night he would wake screaming of some evil that haunted his dreams, dreams which he could not repeat to me. He did appear to brighten at the birth of our son, Daniel, but it was only after Lord Pearl passed away that Winston actually become more his old self."

"Lord Pearl died? Of natural causes?" Holmes asked.

"Oh yes. The doctor said he had been ill for some time. His heart, you see. I was assuming that was why he sent for Winston to return home."

"I see. So now you became Lord and Lady of the manor?"

"Yes. Lord Pearl left a will but the entire holdings were not given to Winston. They were left to our son. Winston was merely to act as administrator until Daniel became of age to inherit in his own right."

"And what of Daniel? How old is he now?" Holmes asked.

The room became deathly still and the blood drained from Dorthea Pearl's face. She struggled to hold back the tears that filled her eyes when she looked at Holmes. She had feared and dreaded the moment when she would have to reveal the truth. Her lips moved and formed words but her only sound was a wrenching sob so agonizing and painful that it tore at both Holmes and Watson. Unable to face Sherlock Holmes, but more intolerable was knowing the look of pity that was in Watson's eyes, she buried her face in her hands and the words poured forth piteously.

"That's my turmoil, my agony, Mr. Holmes!" she cried. "You see that's just my turmoil! Daniel is dead! Daniel is dead and so is Winston! I have been going mad these past several months since the accident and I fear I am losing my mind. I see Winston sometimes in the night, in the dark, he calls to me, he beckons me to come to him. He wishes me to be with him and knowing the pain and grief suffered by my father after my mother's death, I cannot help but feel that it would be better if I were to join Winston. My Daniel was taken from me. He was the light of my life. I see him also, Mr. Holmes. He is there in the night calling to me, Mama! Mama! Help me Mama! And I cannot help him, Mr. Holmes because I cannot reach him! And this loss of Cousin Agnes…it is all simply too much!" Dorthea sobbed into her handkerchief.

Shocked by Dorthea's sudden anguished confession Watson stared at the sobbing woman and went to kneel beside her.

"There, there now. Dorthea. Crying into hysteria will do no good. You must calm yourself. I can give you something if you wish?"

Dorthea accepted a clean handkerchief from Holmes, and dabbed her eyes. "I apologize, I really do. I did not wish to break down as I did, but I have lost both my Winston and Daniel and now they call to me. I desperately need your help, Mr. Holmes. I have been so alone in my loss these few months, not knowing who to trust, where to turn, who to believe. I am at a loss as to what to do, or where to turn. They are there in the night calling to me, coming to me in dreams that I cannot stop! Please can you help?"

"You have not been to a doctor?"

"Oh yes, the local doctor and my friend, Dr. Leonard Farley. He tells me it is natural and it happens to many women after such a tragedy. But I cannot believe him, Mr. Holmes. They are so real, as if they are still here with me!" she cried.

Watson put his arm about Dorthea and handed her a fresh handkerchief once more. "For pity's sake, Holmes!" he glared at him. "Give the woman a moment to regain herself!"

"Yes, of course, Watson. When you have calmed down, Lady Pearl, I must ask you questions. I need you to answer them as bravely and honestly as you can. I understand your situation, believe me I do. But right now, what I really need you to do is calm yourself and perhaps we can get down to the matter of this."

"Yes, oh yes. I will do what you ask, Mr. Holmes. I am so sorry, John. I should have given you some sort of indication of my situation perhaps you would not have been so ready to offer me assistance."

"Nonsense, my dear, there is nothing I would not do to help you. Here, a fresh cup of hot tea. There's a touch of brandy so sip it slowly and take several deep breaths. There. That is much better. Do you feel up to Holmes asking questions? There are times when he is an obnoxious, overbearing inquisitor, but he is correct. The questions must be asked and you must answer as truthfully as you can."

"Yes, I do apologize once more. Go ahead, Mr. Holmes, I will try to answer as best as I can."

"First I need to know when Daniel was born."

"Daniel was born eight years ago. We made Gray Manor our home despite Winston's father. It was some time before I was myself again after the birth and Winston felt we should remain, at least until I was better. But by that time, we had settled in somewhat. Lord Pearl was ill the entire time we lived there. Winston felt that now that he himself was a father, he owed it to his own father to stay and put things to right. But Lord Pearl, as ill as he was, wanted nothing to do with Winston or myself. The only one he would see routinely was Daniel. He grew to be quite close to Daniel."

"I see. And Lord Pearl? When did he die?"

"Three years ago."

"So Daniel was five at the time. I see. And what was the accident that took your son's and husband's life and when was that?"

Dorthea closed her eyes. She could feel the presence of John sitting near her, and it gave her comfort. She took a deep breath before she felt confident enough to answer without breaking down. "Three months ago. Winston took Daniel out fishing and when they did not return by nightfall, a search party was formed."

"He …we would always spend our Sunday after services near the water having a picnic. I would usually read while Winston and Daniel swam in the water or went fishing. But that day I was not feeling well and had stayed home. They found…." Dorthea closed her eyes, her lips trembled. Feeling Watson's reassuring hand grasp hers once more, she swallowed before answering, "They found Winston's body three days later on the beachhead. He'd been swept down the coast by the tide and I was told he was badly disfigured from the rocks."

"So you did not personally identify the body?"

"No. Dr. Farley felt it better if I did not. He said it was no sight for a woman to look upon. Dr. Farley was the family doctor for years and the only practitioner in Cadwith so he was able to identify Winston for me. He did have me verify the clothing and the ring that Winston wore on his little finger. It was the ring of his family crest, you see."

"And what of your son? What of Daniel?"

"Dan…Daniel was never found. The fishermen believed that his body was so slight that the tide took him out and…and…that he would possibly never be found…and I feel it is so much my fault….that I should have gone that day…that if I had only been there this would not have happened….I should have been there!"

"Don't blame yourself, Dorthea. Whether you were there or not, you mustn't blame yourself," Watson soothed.

"Watson is right, of course. The blame does not lie with you, Lady Pearl. But let's continue, shall we? The estate? How is it situated financially?"

"That's just it, Mr. Holmes. Once Lord Pearl passed and the will was read, Winston found the estate to be worth more than five hundred thousand pounds! It was a fortune! Why was he living as though he had nothing? We could not understand this. But the will provided for Winston to manage the estate with a ten thousand pound allowance per year until such time as our s...son would come of age."

"Did your husband find that sum sufficient to manage the estate?"

"Of course! Ten thousand pounds is a grand sum of money and not only could we manage to run the estate, we also managed to hire more help and bring the place up to the old standards. You must remember, Mr. Holmes, that Gray Manor owns everything for miles and the rents that come in from the tenants are generous."

"When exactly had Lord James Pearl died?"

"It was three years ago. Three years ago to this very month."

"I see. And the fishing accident was three months ago? That is very interesting."

"In what way, Holmes?" Watson asked.

"Just interesting, Watson. So how did the village of Cadwith respond to having Winston managing the estate?"

"Oh let me tell you they were joyous over Lord James Pearl's death. He was such a tyrant to them you see. As far as Winston, they were very skeptical of him at the first, Mr. Holmes. The older ones remembered Winston from his childhood and tended to be more forgiving of the Pearl name, but the younger people tended to be very wary of him believing him to be like his father. But when Winston discovered he could manage the estate very well on the allotted amount of money, well…it was about a year ago that he reduced the rents from the tenants on the estate lands as well as taking a smaller share of the crops and fishing incomes. He was also able to provide money for renovations to the church in the village. That seemed to bring the whole community around and they immediately were drawn to him. Winston was a kind and generous man, Mr. Holmes. He was honest and fair and resented that his father had been so cruel and demanding of them."

"I see."

"But it was only several months later that Winston's first accident occurred," Dorthea said, wiping her eyes once more.

"There was an accident?" asked Watson

"A first accident?" Holmes asked casting Watson a quick look.

"Yes. There were two now that I recall. It was nearly four months after reducing the rents that Winston was injured. As an engineer he was appalled at the state of the buildings but because his father was still alive and was still in charge of the estate, there was not much Winston could do except some minor repairs. Even those he had to goad Lord Pearl into the repairs siting a safety issue… for Daniel you see. But once Lord Pearl passed, he threw himself enthusiastically into the estate and had undertaken a massive renovation project.

"He was immediately his old self once more, Mr. Holmes. Whistling and humming as he planned and worked with Daniel at his side nearly all the time. Most times underfoot, but Winston never seemed to mind or tire of his endless questions and mischievousness. He began with the west wing of the house and rectified the loose railings and banisters as well as any other areas of construction that were faulty. He also hired gardeners to make a clean sweep of the grounds trimming, cutting and setting in new plantings and ridding the front of the house of that horrid crumbling rock wall.

"The area near the Gray Mausoleum was in a tragic state of neglect and it was there one day that one of the statues on a pedestal toppled over. It knocked Winston to the ground pinning his leg, but with the help of the others, the statue was removed. Winston's injuries were slight. It made him more determined to repair the area before anyone, especially our Daniel, could possibly be hurt. It was a setback for him because he had only been able to restore the west wing when the accident occurred. He so wished to repair the east wing but the fallen statue convinced him that the mausoleum grounds required his attention first."

"I see. And the second incident?"

"It occurred some three months after that. All the entrances to the east wing were sealed off years ago by Lord Pearl and no one was ever allowed to go there. Winston found a ring of keys beneath a stack of books in the library one day and found that one of the keys fit a door to the east wing and he alone went in, in case it proved too dangerous for passage. When he opened the door, we saw a stair case to one side and then a long corridor. Along both sides after that were rooms with all the doors closed. At the end of the corridor was a set of doors which opened up to an outside veranda. That was boarded up from the inside. He did not dare trust the wood and came back, deciding instead to mount the stairs to the second floor of the wing. He was nearly to the top when he said a rotted stair gave way. This time I was truly worried because Winston had fallen through and tumbled the length of the stairs. He was unconscious for quite some time and remained bed ridden for days crying out about the shadows in the darkness, of the white witch that haunts there still. Dr. Farley said it was a severe concussion and he must remain calm for at least one week."

"Did Winston return to the east wing once recovered?"

"No, he decided to put off the renovations for a later date. It was as if something about that wing of the house frightened him, Mr. Holmes. Afterwards, he simply refused to talk about it further. He locked the door once more and hid the keys."

"I did notice you said earlier that your cook is Justine yet when you and your husband arrived at Gray Manor you stated Elizabeth was the cook?"

"Yes, that is correct. After Daniel was born, Winston convinced Lord Pearl that the house badly needed some repair and cleaning. Reluctantly the old man agreed, for the benefit of Daniel. More staff were hired and he agreed with Winston to retire Jessop and Elizabeth. They had been with the Pearl's all their lives and were near into their eighties. He gave them a small cottage and a yearly stipend and a small lot for their own. He made sure they are well taken care of. It was only after Lord Pearl died that we were able to hire additional staff and begin to repair the place as it required."

Holmes raised his eyebrows and cast Watson another look. "And since you have been in London visiting your

Cousin Agnes, have you experienced any recurrences of the dreams of seeing Winston and Daniel?"

At that, Dorthea once more uttered a sob and the tears streamed down her cheeks. "Oh yes, Mr. Holmes! But…but they aren't dreams! They are…they are…real! I see him, Mr. Holmes! In my sleep and in my waking moments! I see them both! They appear and then are gone. They appear and call to me and when I try to follow, they are gone as quickly as they appeared. I am so ashamed to admit that I am seeing their spirits, their ghosts. I never knew such a thing to be possible but it is true for it is happening to me!

"It appears that I cannot rid myself of the images and cries for help. I see Winston everywhere! I see him in a crowd of people but he is always just out of reach. I see his face in the windows of the shops when I pass and when I turn he is nowhere to be seen. I hear his voice calling to me sometimes, but I cannot trace where it is coming from. I fear I am losing my mind, Mr. Holmes!"

"Nonsense, Dorthea, dear," Watson said putting an arm about her shoulder. "It is grief and no more than that. Everyone experiences strange events following the death of a dear loved one. Goodness knows you have had more than your share of that. You must not allow yourself to think or feel that way. I am sure with time, your grief will heal and you will become yourself once more."

"But does anyone truly heal after losing a child, John? After losing a husband? Can life truly go on as before…as though the tragedy had not occurred? Can one forget the loss? The pain is so unbearable it tears at my heart stealing its beat until I cannot catch my breath! How does one get past that, John?"

Watson lowered his head and summoned all the courage from deep within. He had not spoken of the tragic loss of his wife, Mary, to anyone. He had not told anyone of his feelings, of his deep depression and loss of will to go on. He told no one because he had no one close enough that he cared to trust or call a true friend. No one because it was at that very same time that he lost his dear friend Sherlock Holmes over the falls at Reichenbach, Switzerland and the devastation of the loss of the two people he held most dear to his heart had been overwhelming.

He looked up and into the pained brown eyes staring at him from a face from the past that he had forgotten to call friend. "I know that one never truly heals, Dorthea, for there will always be that place in the heart and mind that will never stop loving them; never forget them. But I also know that dealing with the loss becomes more tolerable as each day passes because there are always the memories of your love. It is the pain of the loss that reminds us, Dorthea. But as for the rest my dear, I can speak from my own heart. After my wife Mary passed away, I was stricken with the utmost and deplorable grief and found myself lost with no accounting for time or events for days. I wandered aimlessly, blaming myself although there was no blame to be put but I was alone with my grief and it was unbearable. I was inconsolable. But time passed and soon I realized that Mary was still with me… here," Watson placed his hand on his heart. "I came to a peaceful calming inside that finally allowed me to see each day for what it was, a new beginning, a fresh start. There is not a day that goes by that I do not think of Mary. But each of those days my thoughts are of her goodness, her sweetness, her beauty and how she made my life wonderful."

Dorthea wiped her tears and took his hand in hers. "Oh, John, you are such a wonderful friend. I should have come to you sooner. I should have known you would understand. Ambrose was wise to make your acquaintance and wiser still to have brought you home to become my friend. Thank you."

Holmes cleared his throat. "Getting back shall we. One more question for now, Lady Pearl. How long are you intending to stay in London?"

"I am returning the day after tomorrow. My cousin Agnes was laid to rest this past week and I really must return. I have left the care of Gray Manor to our estate manager, Arthur Upland. I have been away from Gray Manor much too long and must return although I go with dread."

"Might I make a suggestion, then. I would like Watson to accompany you back to Gray Manor and stay with you. It will be several days before I close up several cases that I am currently working on before I can join you."

"Then you have decided to help?"

"Of course. This case is very intriguing. Rest assured that Watson will take very good care of you." Holmes rose and retrieved the gloves, bonnet and handbag from the table, clearly indicating that the interview was over. "Now, Watson, if you would kindly see Lady Pearl back, I must see to other business."

"Of course, Holmes. Come Dorthea," Watson said.

"Thank you so much, Mr. Holmes. I look forward to your joining us. I cannot tell you how much you have eased my mind from this burden." Dorthea Pearl gripped Holmes hand warmly.

"You are welcome, Lady Pearl. You stay close to Watson and mind what he tells you. It is for your well-being and all done in your best interest. Good day now."

"Very good, Holmes. I won't be long." Watson closed the door quietly behind him.

Chapter Two

Watson was relieved to see Dorthea safely back at Aunt Agnes' with a much brighter demeanor, yet something deep inside was persistently nudging the back of his mind, despite Holmes' assurance that he would help. He couldn't help the uneasy feeling that had settled in the pit of his stomach over what lay ahead for them at Gray Manor.

Upon his return, he requested a tray be sent to his room, his need to be alone was great. It was some time after the evening meal had been cleared before he decided to go to the study. He'd had enough of trying to make sense of Dorthea's situation.

He closed the door to his private apartment and entered the study where Holmes was sitting near the fireplace, pipe in hand. Gray smoke rose steadily from the burning raggs tobacco. Holmes eyes were closed. It seemed Holmes, once more, had fallen asleep with a lit pipe. Watson stooped to retrieve the pipe from Holmes' fingers when Holmes spoke. "I am awake, Watson. No fear of my pipe. Sit won't you? Your thoughts are much preoccupied. Lady Pearl, I presume?"

"Yes, Holmes, I am afraid that is so. Her situation has been on my mind this entire evening and I am genuinely concerned for her health. Her physical as well as her mental well-being is being compromised with these thoughts of voices and ghosts. Although I may be able to help her with any physical discomforts, I am truly at a loss as to what to do with this imagining of apparitions. Yet today, as I escorted her to the door of her Cousin Agnes' home, I had the most peculiar feeling that we were being followed."

"You were my good man. I could not possibly allow such an opportunity to pass. Once you and Lady Pearl left our apartments, I quickly donned a disguise and started out after you. I did note one point of interest. It appears that not one but two persons were interested in you both. One was an elderly woman in a cab that followed you. She stopped at the corner and watched while you made your goodbyes to Lady Pearl and saw her safely inside. Once done, the elderly woman seemed to think enough of the matter then left. I was not able to identify her features for she was wearing a veil, but the hand that held the curtain to the side of the window was frail and the joints gnarled with age. The skin was wrinkled and her nails short. A woman who has led a hard life to be sure."

"And the second? You said there were two interested parties."

"The second was a younger man disguised as an elderly man, and a very poor disguise I might add. But he did make a very clever attempt to hide the fact that he was following you. He did not arrive on the scene until your cab was two streets from Cousin Agnes. At which point he very awkwardly misused the cane in his right hand as a walking stick because of his limp. I feel sure noone else noticed this discrepancy, but as you know, such errors are so easy for me to detect. This man walked slowly along the fence, stopping now and then to steady himself and once you saw Lady Pearl inside, limped his way to the next street where he turned and continued down the side street with no limp."

"You do not mean the bearded man with the knit cap? I did notice but paid no attention, Holmes."

"Which is why you have me, Watson."

"What do you make of it?"

"I am not sure as of yet, but one thing I do know is that apparitions do not don disguises and follow someone down the streets of London let alone follow someone from Cornwall to London. I believe Lady Pearl to be in danger. I do not know why or who just yet. But I do know I want you to accompany her back to Gray Manor and stay with her. Never leave her out of your sight. I will close up the mariner case and will be there as soon as I am able."

"That I will do, Holmes."

"Has everything been arranged for your departure?"

"Yes. I've booked us passage out on the twelve o'clock train. That will give us more than a seven hour ride west stopping at Great Torrington in Devon. I've wired ahead and reserved rooms at the Galloping Pony, a small inn there. The following morning we will ride by coach to Cadwith. Dorthea has sent word ahead to have her groomsman waiting for us there. I fear it will be a long and exhausting journey for her, but she wished to make the extension to Great Torrington to show me some of the Cornish countryside. I could not refuse her that. That poor woman has suffered greatly these past few months," Watson sighed.

"I am suspecting that you owe her for some past debt, Watson?"

"Yes….no…well not her exactly." Watson rose to fill his pipe. He took purposefully long in filling and packing the tobacco before lighting it, his back to Holmes. Thoughts of Ambrose came to mind and he closed his eyes in a futile attempt to block them out.

"I am waiting, Watson."

"I do not know that I wish to speak of it, Holmes. It holds tragic memories you see."

"I cannot imagine the horrible ordeal your friend Dorthea Pearl has been through these past few months, yet she found the courage to speak of it, Watson," Holmes goaded his friend.

Watson's turned with a sudden anger upon Holmes. This intrusion by Holmes into his past, his private loss, his unbearable guilt had been imminent the entire day. He seethed and sputtered, unable to utter the words that raced through his mind. Whirling away from the fireplace, he paced from the chair to the window and back, his footsteps falling heavily on the floor. "You simply must know, mustn't you? You're simply not happy until you know everything! All right! All right then. It is probably better if I speak of it for it haunts me still."

"Perhaps it would be better if you poured us a brandy and sat down."

Once more Watson cast Holmes an angry glare. He knew it would come to this sooner or later. The meeting with Dorthea Pearl had opened all the painful wounds of loss that had flooded Watson's thoughts all day. Losses that had been his and his alone for all these years and now were being brought out into the open by Sherlock Holmes, intruded upon by his own inner guilt, a guilt he had lived with and tucked away in the back of his brain so long ago. He poured two glasses of brandy, slopping the darkened liquid on the mantle and after shoving a glass at Holmes, went to sit. He took several gulps, half emptying his glass before taking a deep breath.

"It was years ago, when I entered the military service. There are times it seems as if it was a life time ago and other times it feels as if that life belonged to someone else. There are times it feels as if it were only yesterday and the memories are so real, so haunting. Yet at other times I must struggle to remember them. I do not know which is worse. I have been thinking all day that I can understand the horrors that Dorthea is going through for I went through much the same." He took another deep swallow and continued.

"Because of my medical training I was transferred to the Army Medical Department of the 66th Foot. I received additional training and was assigned as assistant surgeon to Dr. Bernard Blethley who was, by my estimation, one of the most excellent surgeons of our time. We spent hours together both in and out of the field and I found Blethley to have a natural feel for surgery. His perception and response when assessing a patients' needs was exceptional. His sensitivity and compassion of a patients' well-being as well endeared him to every man in our company. It was there also that I met Ambrose Kippford and we grew to be good friends.

"Once the war broke out in the British holdings in the middle east, our troop was dispatched and soon we were in the thick of it. It was always a constant battle, Holmes. The pushing forward, pursuing the enemy. The explosions of weapons, the roar of war, and always the pain of the wounded, the dying. Then there was the intolerable heat with its incessant sand and wind, the lack of water, little hygiene. It was never ending. We were under the leadership of Captain William Roberts who was an able and capable leader. We saw fighting at Arzu and Charasiab. On both occasions we held ground and maintained our hold. Sometimes only just. We had many casualties but as long as our triumphs maintained, the troops were willing to follow him into yet another battle. It wasn't until the battle at Maiwand that we finally met defeat. And what a horrific defeat that was.

"For days we fought, pushed forward, were pushed back, taking ground, losing ground. The battle was raging, hellacious for both sides. We were outnumbered more than ten to one but Captain Roberts would not retreat. He was a proud and dedicated soldier. All for the crown, you know. He ordered the men to stand and hold and that they did; or at least tried to do. Dr. Blethley and I were in the medical arena and the dead and wounded poured in like rain drops on a stormy day. Except it wasn't rain it was bullets and it wasn't a storm it was a war. Most of the men had been shot and bayoneted so many times that there was nothing we could do for them but give them morphine for the pain. Soon even that ran out. We were being overrun faster than we could run and we lost so many men……so many men." Watson emptied his glass and absent mindedly, rose to refill his. He stood staring into the fire.

"That day….that final day….we could hear the battle raging closer. It was so close the ground actually shook beneath our feet. There was the screaming and the shouting and it was deafening. There was no definition as to line of battle, no differentiation as to war zone or medical zone. Our tents were under constant fire now and on more than one occasion the bullets tore holes through the canvas. We worked furiously on the wounded, but we simply could not keep up.

"There was no more room in the tents. We were piling the dead outside. It seemed the rows went on and on and on and we had no place left to put them. The bullets were now such a constant barrage over our heads that we were working on hands and knees. The ground was covered in blood, my own clothes, my knees, my hands, everything was soaked in it. It was impossible to determine whether one was bleeding from a wound or saturated with the blood of others.

"I was assisting a poor lad who was bayoneted through his skull when Ambrose Kippford staggered into the tent and collapsed nearby, his head bleeding profusely. I immediately tore strips from his torn and bloody shirt to bind his head wound because we had depleted our store of bandaging hours before. The medicines were gone, the bandaging was gone, the clean water was gone. Before I was even through tying the knot, shots rang throughout the tent and I saw Dr. Blethley fall. He had been mortally shot in the chest and was dead immediately. It was but a few volleys later that I was shot through my shoulder and was thrown to the ground barely conscious.

"I do not know how Ambrose did it, but with the help of my orderly, they managed to get hold of me and drag me from the tent. I remember the excruciating pain and the blood streaming out of my body as we dodged enemy fire. I felt I was leaving a trail of blood for the enemy to find us. I remember shouting at them to leave me and save themselves, but they refused. I soon became delirious from the pain and have no recollection of anything after that. I do know that Ambrose risked his life to save mine. We managed to make it through the enemy lines and hide in safety, traveling at night until we could reach our own lines. It was several days later that we were almost killed by our own men before we were recognized and taken in to safety.

"I lay in hospital for weeks out of my head with a fever on my brain and an infection in my shoulder that appeared would never cease. When I finally opened my eyes, the first face I saw before me was Ambrose. Weeks had already passed and his head wound was nearly healed. He was once again on his way into battle. He had been temporarily reassigned to Major General Sir Patrick Reilly and they were on the march to Kandahar.

"It....it was nearly a year later that I finally was able to face the world once more and traveled to St. Stephens to visit my old friend. He'd sent me a letter saying he'd recently returned home from the war and I simply had to come. He introduced me to Winston Pearl, Dorthea's husband, and who was by now, excited for the birth of their up-coming child.

"There was some sort of festival going on at the time. I do not recall exactly what it was for and it makes no never mind. But during the course of the festivities a fight ensued and several of the towns people got into a heated argument over the tunnels in the mine. Soon there were guns involved. Ambrose, who was a completely innocent bystander, was shot at nearly point blank range with an old musket. The ball penetrated his chest cavity and entered his lung. It was such a huge hole! And bleeding ......I couldn't stop the bleeding!

"Damn it, Holmes! The man dragged and carried me through hell and saved my life yet when it was my turn...my...my turn to repay the debt, there was nothing I could do. Nothing I could do, Holmes! I tried to stop the bleeding but his lung was already filling with blood. It was running out of his mouth and he could barely breathe. I held him in my arms and all I could do was whisper 'I'm sorry old friend' while the tears fell from my eyes, and I felt his last breath slip away." Watson went to the window to conceal his distress from Holmes.

"I am so very sorry, Watson," Holmes whispered into the silence.

In the penetrating sorrow that filled the room, the only sound was the ticking of the clock on the fireplace mantle. Holmes reached to relight his pipe then put his feet on the ottoman and closed his eyes. Watson remained near the window staring into the streets below yet seeing nothing. Time slipped by and Watson leaned his head against the cool of the window pane as the images of the past came flooding through. Images of he and Ambrose playing croquet with Dorthea on the emerald grasses of St. Stephens, her laughter like the song of a bird on the wind. Images of Ambrose staggering into the medical tent, the blood streaming down his face. Images of Ambrose struggling while he gripped Watson beneath his shoulder forcing him to move forward, move to safety. Images of Ambrose lying in his arms, blood running from the corner of his mouth, assuring Watson that everything was all right. Images of a friendship that comes to a person only once in a lifetime, never to be had again. Slowly the images faded and Watson came to with a start. He shrugged away the stirred memories, then poured two fresh glasses of brandy.

"I have not seen Dorthea all these years since his death. I simply could not face her."

"Surely she did not blame you?"

"No…no of course not. She was there with me, she saw the situation and understood that there was nothing I could do. Still….all these years I have lived with an inner guilt that I should have been able to do something, anything to save my friend's life."

"You are too hard on yourself, Watson. I am sure Ambrose knew that you were doing all that could be done. I am sure Ambrose was grateful to have had you there with him at the end, a good friend."

"Perhaps you are correct. Perhaps all these years I have blamed myself for my inability to save his life when I should have placed the blame on the man who fired the shot. He was hanged, of course. His death did not lessen the pain of Ambrose's death. Yet, I should be consoled in that justice had been served."

"Yes. Speaking of justice. You must not blame yourself any further, Watson. Now you must channel your energy and thoughts into taking care of your friend Dorthea Pearl until we have resolved the case."

Watson swallowed the last of the brandy in his glass. "You are right, of course, Holmes," he said with a choking sadness. "You always are." He turned and left, closing the door to his private apartments behind him.

Holmes leaned back, alone now in the quiet study, drawing heavily on his pipe, blowing the smoke in swirling clouds towards the ceiling. His thoughts drifted over the details of the battle of Maiwand according to Watson's perspective; no, according to Watson's experience. To be at the forefront and a witness as well as a casualty to the horrific battles of death and destruction of human life. He thought back to those cases where Watson appeared to hold back when the cause for a weapon came to use, thought about his cautious handling of the thing, and the reticence displayed whenever a shot was inevitable. He thought back to Watson's determined insistence to know and learn all he could about the man called Sherlock Holmes. A man that, after some time, Watson called friend. He thought about Watson's persistent nagging of him to quit the practice of using narcotics to stimulate himself during those lethargic, depressing days when no interesting case was at hand.

Holmes thought about Ambrose, a man who had been close to Watson, had saved his life and died in his arms. He thought of Watson's self- blame and the guilt he thrust upon himself and lived with all these long years.

Throughout his life, he, Holmes, had never really had a close friend, someone he would risk his life for or he for him. Not until Watson. Their relationship had grown from two people sharing expenses and living quarters to that of a trusted colleague and true friend. Yes, Watson was indeed a man Holmes called a friend. Now he understood a small portion of the quiet doctor who plunged himself wholeheartedly into saving those about him that he considered friend. Holmes thought of all those times and a new and profound respect for Watson came to him.

Chapter Three

Departure day arrived and Watson and Dorthea Pearl were on their way to the train station. A soft gentle rain tapped the top of the cab but did nothing to relieve the stifling heat of the day. A storm was brewing.

The station was bustling with people already in a hurry with their comings and goings so they quickly found their compartment and boarded. He stowed their bags in the overhead storage, then sat opposite Dorthea. She was gazing out the window and although he wanted to interrupt her he felt the intruder. He reached for a newspaper but his mind was lost in thought about what awaited them at Gray Manor.

Not a moment had passed after Watson's departure before Holmes set to work. A few minor alterations in his dress and facial features and he was out on the street. He arrived at the station several minutes later and with a quick glance about, he saw them. Discretely remaining out of sight, he watched from a platform beneath the glazed roof, behind the wrought iron arches. There were hundreds of people and children milling about waiting for the train, but he did not see anyone in particular following them. He cursed under his breath. The people following Dorthea Pearl were, in all probability, already on the train. He jumped aboard just as the train began to depart.

Their coach was quiet at first until, in the awkward silence, both began to speak at the same time. They laughed and Watson said, "Go ahead, you first."

"I was going to say how grateful I am that Sherlock Holmes has decided to help me and that you are accompanying me back to Gray Manor. The weight that has been lifted from me is enormous."

"I am happy to be at your service, my dear. As for Holmes, I knew that although his objections appear most adamant when anyone *tells* him what to do, the moment he heard your situation he would throw himself in wholeheartedly."

"Is that what happened? You told him to help?"

"No, not at all! I simply stated you were coming and that he should pay particular attention to your situation as he would be helping regardless whether he wished so or not."

Dorthea laughed. "John you are such a dear. It was a blessed day when we met again. Already the terrifying horror of the last several months has diminished. Knowing you and Mr. Holmes are here to help has relieved my anxieties greatly."

"Then I am happy." Their eyes met briefly until the awkward moment was broken when Watson once more turned to his newspaper. He thought back to Holmes' final words before departure, 'always carry your service revolver, Watson. Always.' Feeling the bulge of the weapon at the inside of his coat pocket, Watson breathed a sigh of relief. He turned the pages of the newspaper and soon was absorbed in the day old news that he had not the opportunity to read until now.

Dorthea reached into her handbag for a small book and the lazy afternoon slowly waned into evening. The skies remained dark and clouded, the storm threatening but not yet forthcoming. An omen, Watson thought, of what was perhaps to come at Gray Manor? Watson's stomach rumbled.

"My goodness!" Dorthea looked up from her book. "I do believe it might be time to eat?"

"I certainly agree. The time has slipped away quickly. Either that or our reading material was immensely interesting. Come. Let us go in search of the dining car."

They made their way carefully along the narrow corridor stopping on more than one occasion to allow others to pass. The cars swayed gently to the rhythm of the wheels on the track and they matched the movement as they passed from coach to coach before arriving at the dining compartment. They entered from the vestibule and saw that it was not yet full. A narrow corridor ran the length of the coach and in the center was partitioned an area that housed the galley.

A table near the end of the coach was unoccupied. Watson and Dorthea sat there where they would have some privacy. He sat with his back to the coach so Dorthea need not be concerned or afraid of being exposed. Ahead, he could see his reflection in the window, muted and gray like the weather outside. One of the wait staff was at their table with a swift bow and a fresh pot of tea and taking their meal requests.

Watson smiled across the table at Dorthea. "You are smiling."

"Yes, I am happy you are with me, John," she said. She unfolded the napkin and reached for her tea.

"As am I to be here, Dorthea. Soon we will be arriving in Great Torrington. I have heard the Galloping

Pony has wonderful accommodations. Our rooms are across from each other so if you should need me during the night, I will be close at hand."

"I am sure everything will be just fine, John."

"And your sleep last night? Thank you," Watson said to the waiter who set their plates to the table. "Was it comfortable?"

"Yes, as a matter of fact, I have been having difficulty falling to sleep as of late, but last night was quiet."

"I am glad of it. Should you need something to help you, let me know. I dislike the use of narcotics, but sometimes they are essential to the well-being of the patient."

"So," Dorthea's eyebrows arched, "now I am to be your patient?"

"Oh no! I simply meant…"

"John," she laughed and placed a hand over his, "do not fret yourself, I am toying with you. It has been some time since I have been able to laugh. Thank you for that."

"I do not mind at all. There is no offense between friends, Dorthea. Would you care for something stronger than the tea?"

"No, it is only an hour or so and we shall be snug in our beds at the Galloping Pony and I am hoping tonight remains as quiet as the last."

"I pray it does, also," Watson said. He searched her face for a moment longer as she bent to her food. His gaze wandered toward the window, at the countryside speeding by all blurry up close, but in perfect focus at a distance. He thought how much life was like that. While one is living it, things appear to be moving fast, blurry and out of focus, hard to pinpoint and difficult to grasp. But from a distance, as one ages, the focus becomes more clear. He wondered if that was because one already knew the outcome, because one had already lived through it. If one only could know then what he knows now, what changes in choices there would have been!

"You seem lost in thought," Dorthea said. She moved her empty soup dish to the side.

"I was merely thinking…you know…of the past."

"I see."

"No, not in that respect. Not Ambrose, well, yes Ambrose amongst many other things. You see, Dorthea, I have lived these past years blaming myself for his death despite the fact that I was not the cause of it. I have always felt that I should have been able to do more. And I was so bloody helpless. But now, seeing you again, rekindling all those terrible memories, it has made me look once more at them.

"I have lived in self- condemnation all these years and could not see the damage I was doing both to myself and to you. All these years! Seeing you again has brought up all those horrid memories, but it has brought the good times and good memories back also. I had forgotten those days of fishing and swimming with you and Ambrose at St. Stephens. I had forgotten the three of us walking along the beaches, enjoying picnics and dancing like fools while your Cousin Agnes played the piano. I had forgotten how to laugh. I had forgotten all those good times by dwelling on the sadness and I have missed out on so much! You have shown me the light, Dorthea. I hope that I can do the same for you now….or when you feel it is right."

"I know you wish to help, John, and I want you to know that your being here means more to me than you can ever know. I understand about Ambrose. I have

47

always understood. I understand why you stayed away all those years and I have never held it against you. I know how close you and Ambrose were and now...with Winston and Daniel....I can truly tell you I understand your loss for I am living it once more. I know there will come a time when I see things as you do now. But it will take time. I hope you understand that."

"I do my dear. I only wish there was something I could do to ease your pain. I know it is the sort of pain one must bare alone, until such time that the good memories far exceed those of the bad. A time when one can look back in love and fondness of those times and not in sadness, despair or blame. Your time will come. You are strong and beautiful, Dorthea, and your time will come."

"Thank you John. Your friendship means so much to me."

"As yours is to me. Ah, I think we are approaching Great Torrington. Perhaps we should return to our compartment and see to our bags?"

"Let us give it just a few more minutes. The porters will see to the bags. We still have time."

They sipped the last of their tea in silence while the train slowed to a stop at the small town of Great Torrington. Watson looked off once more into the settling dark of evening, at the shadows thrown by the gas street lamps and was relieved that he had spoken to Dorthea of the darkness that had enveloped him those last few years. Perhaps now the guilt would fade. Perhaps the shadows would fade. It was time to move on.

Very few people alighted and the station house was dark and quiet but for the hissing of the train. Standing on the platform holding their bags they waited for the train to depart. A man stumbled from the last car onto the platform. He rolled and struggled back to his feet, weaving along the platform. He bumped into Watson, drinking from his bottle of rum, then staggered off. Watson gave the man a dismayed look and retrieved his fallen bag. He and Dorthea walked the short distance to the inn where they were escorted to their rooms.

Now alone in his room, his thoughts turned once more to Dorthea's situation and all the horrible details flooded his mind. That same persistent niggling of impending danger prickled the hairs on the back of his neck and he wondered what darkness lay in wait for them at Gray Manor. Darkness and ghosts! Good grief! He thought to himself before pulling the drapes closed. He walked across the hall and gave a light knock.

Footsteps padded across the floor and Dorthea whispered through the door, "Yes?"

"It is John, Dorthea. Is everything all right? Is the room comfortable enough?"

She opened the door with a smile. "Oh yes, the room is fine, John. I am going to wash up and go straight to bed."

"All right then. I shall just be across the hall if you need me. Goodnight then."

"Good night, John."

The old man leaning against the lamp post watched the lights in Dorthea Pearl's room go out. He scraped the smoldering end of the cigar off, tucked the stub into his pocket, and pulled out his small bottle of rum once more. Pulling up the collar of his tattered coat, he cast another glance at the window and drew long on the neck of the bottle. He corked it, tucked it back into his pocket and curled into a ball, pulling the old coat about him and went to sleep.

Watson rose early, washed and dressed then stood in the hall for some minutes before giving a light tap to Dorthea's door. "Dorthea?" he called. He heard the shuffle of feet moving swiftly on the floor.

"Yes?" she called.

"It's me again, John. We have about an hour before our coach arrives. I will meet you downstairs for breakfast then?"

"Yes of course, John. I'll just be a minute. Order for me, would you?"

"Very good." Watson noted the tone of her voice and smiled to himself. She sounded more relaxed and he hoped his visit would see her back to her old self once more. Ten minutes passed before she finally arrived in the small restaurant of the hotel.

"My, my you look bright and chipper this morning," Watson said. He held her chair and nodded to the waiter who arrived quickly with plates of eggs, toasted bread and chunks of steaming ham and tomatoes.

"Oh this looks delicious! And thank you, John. I feel so much better today. To tell you the truth, last night was the first night that I actually slept soundly. No waking to voices, no….no…spirits to torment my dreams. I can't remember the last time I…"

Watson gave her hand a squeeze. "Never mind, I know what you are trying to say. Let it suffice you had a good night's rest and here you are refreshed to start a new day. A bright sunny one I might add. Shall we?" he indicated the food.

"Yes of course. This place is marvelous don't you agree? It is so quaint with those large wood beams. I was told it was built sometime during the 1600's and all of this is original. I just think it is so lovely."

"I see you are becoming versed in the different periods of architecture," Watson said.

"I owe it all to Winston. He is a natural where architecture is concerned. Of course being an engineer I would imagine he would be."

"Yes, I would imagine."

"But once we are on our way, the coach ride is about four hours and we will pass through some of the most beautiful countryside you have ever seen, John Watson. Cornwall is noted for its moors, mist and its treacherous rocky cliff sides and it is lovely there. In the spring when the heather blooms, it smells so clean and fresh. It is one of the things I love about Gray Manor. Gray Manor you know is set not too far from the moors on the one side and the cliffs of the sea on the other. In the early evening when the mist is swirling and the moon is rising.....well, you can see how the horror of Shelley's Frankenstein would come to mind."

"It does sound lovely and I can hardly wait. Perhaps you would be kind enough to show me around? I would like to walk the moors and beaches and learn more of this Gray Manor of yours."

"Of course I will, anything you wish to see. We will make arrangements. Now, let us finish our breakfast for the coach will soon be here."

"You do know, of course, that Torrington is the site of the first battle of our English Civil War. It was a fight between the Royalists, those supporters of King Charles the First and the Parliamentarians. It was presumed to have lasted four years with the culmination of the war and the final battle held here at Great Torrington," said Watson.

"I see you are up on your war battles."

"Of course. This one was particularly important because it saw the end of the Royalist party and the continuation of the Parliament running the government. Although the outcome was partially due to an accident rather than the strategic efforts and military might of the Parliamentarians. You see a spark of fire ignited the old Torrington church where the Royalists, in their insanity of suppositions that nobody ever desecrates a church, stored their cache of gunpowder there. It was, of course, attacked and set afire which apparently set off such an explosion that it killed nearly all the Royalist troops, handing the victory to the Parliamentarians. A stroke of luck for all of us British descendants I might add. Of course the downfall was that a monarch of the British throne was executed but that has happened numerous times through our history not to mention the fact that there were monarchs that should have not been on the throne of England at all."

"Are you a history fanatic, John."

"I don't consider myself so, but I enjoy keeping abreast of news that is old as well as new. There is much to learn from what has happened in the past, Dorthea."

"I daresay there is. But while you men are enthralled by exciting battles of the past, I will enjoy my tranquil countryside. I understand Torrington is surrounded by hills of rolling green and sharp cliffs that drop sheer to the water. Somewhat like our Cadwith. I only wish we had time to view them. But already our coach approaches."

The thunder of hooves and rumbling wheels echoed against the cobble stone streets, slowing as the coachman eased the team to a stop in front of the Galloping Pony. It was an old and well used carriage that creaked when he jumped down from the box. He gave each of the horses a pat on the neck and entered the building announcing at the door that the coach would be leaving in fifteen minutes. He then took himself to the kitchen for his morning meal. A young boy from the stable yard across the way hustled forward with a bucket of water dragging from each hand sloshing more water to the ground than was left in the bucket. The horses drank greedily of the fresh cool water and hung their heads, shifting their weight to one side to rest. Large brown eyes widened as one of the horses tossed her head and eyed the boy, nudging his shoulder. He laughed and drew out a lump of sugar for each then pulled the brush from his pocket and quickly gave each of the Welsh cobs a quick brush down.

The coachman hustled quickly through from the kitchen once more announcing the departure in just a few minutes. Seeing the big man returning, the young stable boy climbed the coach. As the burly man hoisted the luggage above his head and onto the imperial, the boy drew each piece and arranged it neatly securing it all with leather straps then jumped into the coachman's arms.

"There you go, my boy. Nice job. Well done. You been doing as the smithy says?"

"Yes, Papa," the boy grinned and hugged the burly coachman, the scraggy beard tickling his neck.

"Good boy. Mind him now til I get back. Only be another day."

"Yes, Papa, I will."

"Go on now. Off with you." The coachman tapped the boy on the behind sending him back to the smithy's stable yard. He held the door and Dorthea and Watson stepped inside.

They seated across from each other and were soon joined by an elderly woman who sat next to Watson and her nurse who sat next to Dorthea. The last to board was the old man from the train who smelled of stale rum and cigar smoke. He stumbled into the coach, lurching back and forth before finally settling beside Dorthea Pearl, the tattered remnants of his dirty coat brushing against her as he rummaged through his pockets until he had the rum bottle in his grasp.

Dorthea raised her eyes to Watson and looked out the window before the worried look on her face was noticed by the other passengers.

"Sorry m'lady," the old man mumbled. "No harm done?"

"No there is no harm done good sir."

"My name is Beatrice Kendall and this is my nurse, Miss Reglis," the old woman sitting next to Watson offered. "We are not traveling far. I have only come to visit the hospital here. My health, you know. I must have a nurse with me at all times you see. My condition warrants that. We are only going as far as Dorset. Only a two hour journey yet my nurse I must have. You understand, of course."

"Yes, of course. I am Dorthea Pearl and this is my good friend John Watson."

"Good to make your acquaintance, Miss Kendall. I do hope the journey has not been too difficult on your condition?" Watson queried.

"It's Mrs... Mrs. Kendall, long ago widowed. And my condition is very ...well...very delicate. So much so that I can hardly speak of it. Thank goodness I have found a most excellent nurse in Miss Reglis. I simply do not know what I would do without her. And you?" she turned her attention to the old man. "What brings you traveling this way?"

"Me?" the old man mumbled. He rubbed his eyes with the back of his dirty hands, spilling rum as he did so. "Dunno as it's any of your business."

"My goodness me!" Mrs. Kendall cried.

"Now, now, Mrs. Kendall," Miss Reglis soothed. "Do not pay attention. Obviously he wishes to be left alone and so we shall. What is your destination, Mrs. Pearl, if I might ask?"

"Gray Manor in Cadwith. I live there."

"Gray Manor, I have not heard of it. But then I do not get out much anymore," Mrs. Kendall sighed. "My condition you know."

Miss Reglis rolled her eyes to Dorthea and smiled. Dorthea gave her a knowing smile back. They settled into silence and after a few minutes, Dorthea removed the small book from her handbag and turned to the light of the window to read. Watson leaned his head back against the seat. He gave the old man in the ragged coat a wary glance from beneath his half-closed eyelids, but seeing that he paid them no attention but stared purposefully out the window, Watson sighed and closed his eyes. He hoped the old man was not going to accompany them too far into their journey.

And then a thought suddenly struck him. The man who was following him that day to Cousin Agnes's house! He then stared at the old man for several long minutes, intent on memorizing every detail of his disguise. He told himself he would keep a watchful eye on the man as long as he was in their company.

The coach stopped at the small town of Dorset where Mrs. Kendall and her nurse left their company. There were no new passengers and the coach departed immediately.

The old man remained huddled near the window of the coach, his only movement was loud guttural snoring when he shifted his position "He does sleep sound," Dorthea remarked when the coach was under way once more.

"Thank the stars for that," Watson said and they both laughed.

They traveled for a time, speaking in hushed tones so as not to disturb their fellow traveler. Watson gave the smelly old man an occasional wary look and finding him still sleeping continued his conversation with Dorthea. They were traveling along a rough stretch of road that had been damaged by heavy rains and not yet been repaired. The road was rocky and potted with holes where the upheaval had eroded the packing and the coach jolted back and forth. The wheels caught in the deep holes, jostling the three inside.

The coachman reined the team to a stop. One of the horses had thrown a shoe and he could hear it clanging against the rocks with each step the horse took. He cursed under his breath, jumped down and was forced to pry the shoe from its remaining nail before any more damage would be done to the hoof. Leading the horses they soon came upon a farmer tending his fields. The old man in the field pulled his team to a stop and went to the coach.

"Lost a shoe?" he called out.

"Yes. Can you tell me where the nearest smithy is?" the driver called back.

"No smithy around these parts for miles. And you won't get there with that horse hauling that load. You'll ruin her for life."

"Yes, I know that," the driver said. Curious as to why they had stopped, Watson got down from the coach.

"What seems to be the matter, sir?" he called out.

"Horse threw a shoe. Can't go on with her like that," the driver answered. "Can you hold them for a few minutes? I want to talk to that farmer there."

"Of course," Watson reached for the halter and one of the cobs nudged his shoulder. "Sorry old girl. I have no sugar for you."

The driver approached the farmer and leaned on the sagging fence. After what appeared to be some haggling, both heads nodded and the farmer returned to his team to unhitch one of the horses and the driver returned to the coach and unhitched his.

"I cannot thank you enough, Mr. Eyre. I'll see to it personally that your Maybelle is returned to you," the coach driver said.

"No need to be worrying about your cob there. She's a mighty fine looking animal and I'll be sure to be taking good care of her. I'll walk her back to my barn and send word to the smithy back in Dorset and have her looked after. Don't you be fretting about her, Mr. Mungrie, she'll be just fine."

Watson returned to the coach while the driver set to work to harness the horse. It was several minutes before he made the adjustment in the harness to accommodate the difference in size from his Welsh cob who stood a mere 15 hands compared to the 17 hands and larger bulk of the Shire plow horse.

Watson told Dorthea, "Horse threw a shoe. He's changed mounts with the farmer there. We might be a bit late getting to Cadwith. Oh!" he exclaimed on finding the old man gone. "What happened to our smelly friend."

"He got out of the coach just after you and has not returned. Did you not see him?"

"No, to tell you the truth I was busy keeping the horses still. But we are leaving and I am afraid he will miss the coach."

"I'm sure he will find a way to get to where he was going," Dorthea smiled.

The driver, Mr. Mungrie, nodded to the old man and smacked the leathers on the horses rumps. They pulled forward, eager to be on the way, but Mungrie held them back He did not know the personality of the big Shire horse or how he would work with his cobs so he stayed cautious and kept them walking. But he had made a deal with the old farmer. Three free coach rides to Dorset for the farmer's wife to do her shopping was a small price to pay to keep his horse from ruin. It took them an extra hour to make their destination. Despite Mungrie's misgivings about the horses, they worked well together without incident.

Chapter Four

It was mid-afternoon before their coach reached the outskirts of Cadwith. The narrow road wound back and forth, twisting between rock and wood, rising slowly but steadily with the height of the cliffs on which the town was built. Small cottages dotted the landscape here and there and soon the coach moved forward from the rough road to the cobbled streets of Cadwith. They pressed on, passing the small one story thatched houses where far to the right Watson could see a stretch of small cottages bumping each other down the terraced slopes on the green topped cliffs that dropped sheer to the water below. A great stretch of water after that, with no end, its gulls screeching overhead and the smell of salt and fish on the wind.

"What a quaint village!" he remarked.

"Yes it is. This was one of the reasons why I wished to make Cadwith my home despite the foreboding of Gray Manor. The village has not changed for nearly two hundred years and neither have the people who live here. Fishing remains their means of living and just every so often you hear the rumors of …..pirates!" Dorthea leaned close to Watson and whispered.

"Pirates! You must be joking!"

"Not in the least, John." She laughed. "This coast is notoriously noted for the smuggling and pirating that went on years ago. If you walk along some of the smaller coves you can still find traces of shipwrecks and the occasional piece of eight."

"Astounding! I would absolutely love to have such an adventure."

"Then it shall be done," Dorthea smiled at him.

"No, no, my dear. I did not intend that you should put yourself in harms way for my entertainment," Watson exclaimed.

"No need to, John. My estate manager, Arthur Upland, lives here in the village and is one of the most knowledgeable sources of information for anything related to Cadwith and its coastline. I am sure he would be more than happy to point out the coves and inlets that would hold the most interest for you. I am told he was originally from Cadwith before leaving to pursue his medical education and had only returned out of his love for the area."

"That is most interesting. And I would enjoy that very much, Dorthea. Ah, here we are. Arrived at last."

The coach halted in front of a small two story thatched cottage, its stone walls and windows screened by a freshly whitewashed stone wall. A small wood sign pounded into the ground on a stake simply stated, 'Coach Office'.

"You will love this village, John, I know you will." Dorthea brushed her wrinkled dress and set her bonnet straight. "Ah, Angus you are here already," she said when a young man pulled open the door.

"Yes, my Lady. I've been waiting for several hours. Wanted to be sure to be here if the coach arrived early, as it sometimes does. Are you wanting to go directly to the manor, or did you wish to have tea first? I can go in and request Miss Townsend to put on the kettle." The young lad, perhaps twenty, put out his arm for Dorthea to steady herself on as she alighted the coach. He was short of stature with a shock of bright red unruly hair that twisted in curls that flew about in the breeze. His eyes were bright green and the smile he gave to Dorthea was one with at least three teeth missing. He was broad chested and bow legged but quick to please and he burst with feverish enthusiasm to please his mistress.

"We shall go directly to the manor, Angus. I would hate to put Miss Townsend out. We've been on the road far too long and I wish to nap this afternoon. I am frightfully tired."

"As you wish, my Lady. I'll just get your bags then. I am sorry my Lady but I brought the trap. One of the carriage wheels was broke a spoke and is in repair."

"That will have to do then, Angus."

"Yes, my Lady."

"Is everything all right, Dorthea?" Watson alighted from the coach.

"Yes that is Angus my stable hand. He sees to the care of the animals and the carriages. He is very good with the animals. A bit slow if you know what I mean but absolutely wonderful with the animals. Come, John. We'll go directly to Gray Manor. We will have a late lunch and perhaps nap."

"Yes, I am rather hungry as well as could use a quiet lie down for a bit." Watson assisted Dorthea into the two seat pony trap while Angus secured their bags to the back. He took in a deep breath. "I do enjoy the fresh smells of the country."

Angus gave the ponies the rein. Accustomed to his gentle hand they ambled slowly along the cobbled street, their hooves a steady clop clop against the stones. Trees thickened and the small cottages disappeared behind them one by one until the cobbled stone of the village gave way to a pebbled road. The road curved and twisted with gentle and easy care, its borders amass with wildflowers growing abundant beneath the shade of the trees.

The ponies worked together when the road sharpened abruptly before them. Angus allowed their gait to slow until they reached the top. Here the tranquility of the old stone cottages of the village was replaced with the suddenness of the dark woods that bordered the road on both sides. Huge trees of pine and oak grew thick and close. The wind blew lightly, rustling the newly sprouted oak leaves, creaking old and tired branches that groaned against the soft sighing of the pine boughs. Giant stumps, old and gray and eroded over time, loomed menacingly through the mist that now crept and swirled through the undergrowth. Deeply trodden animal trails beaten through the forest from years of migrations, crisscrossed the woods, their shadowed portals disappeared into the darkness where the large branches of the giant pines folded onto their edges. Watson shuddered when the coolness of the shade enveloped the trap and Dorthea pulled her shawl closer.

"It's haunted you know," she whispered.

"It is not!" Watson returned quickly. Perhaps too quickly for she had just expressed the very thought that had come to his mind.

"Yes it is. Everyone here talks about it. They say there are ghosts that roam here, the souls of those taken by the sea and never properly buried. There is the one in particular that haunts this forest, a man tall and lean with a long beard that tends to the souls. They are meant, I am sure, to keep the children away for safety reasons because the forest ends abruptly at the top of the cliffs that fall to the sea.

"And that was one problem for Daniel for he was never afraid of this forest. He would ride Magnus, his horse here despite my misgivings and actually venture inside. He said it was so peaceful and quiet there, the only sounds were the birds and the wind in the trees. He loved that forest almost as much as he loved the sea."

"That certainly is the way of young lads isn't it? Brave and without a care. Daniel must have been a wonderful boy," Watson said trying to shake off that unmistakable crawling feeling that they were being watched.

"Oh he is….he was, John." Dorthea stared wistfully into the darkness and whispered, "There are times when we ride here that I believe I can see Daniel still there, riding Magnus happily through the trees. Still see him through the shadowed darkness calling to me, waving to me, beckoning me to come forward."

Watson detected the tremor in Dorthea's voice and changed the subject. "So this forest is just a few miles then we come to that large hill where you said the sight of the manor is so breathtaking?"

"Yes, just around that bend up there. If you look ahead, you can see the sun shining ahead where the forest ends and the sun shine through once more. Angus! Angus!" Dorthea called out.

"Yes my Lady?"

"When we reach the top of the hill, please stop for a moment. I wish my friend to see the manor from here?"

"As you wish, my Lady."

"It is most spectacular, John, especially since Winston has had most of the place restored."

"I can hardly wait."

Once again the ponies leaned into the harness. The road eased into a gradual incline for several yards then rose suddenly, steeply, pulling the weight of the pony trap backward on them. Angus let the reins slip to the seat and without missing a step, jumped from the trap and reached for the harness gently urging them forward. The incline rose at such a sharp pitch, both Watson and Dorthea were compelled to lean backward into the seat.

"I must say this is rather unnerving!" remarked Watson.

Dorthea laughed. "I felt the same way the first few times traveling this road, but once one becomes accustomed to it, it isn't as bad as one first thought."

"Easy there Emma my girl," Angus put his arm about the neck of the pony. "You should be used to this you know. We have traveled this road many times and still you shy. Phillip is pulling more weight than you, you minx. I believe you pretend to be frightened so I will come to your rescue." Angus rubbed Emma's muzzle and she nickered softly nudging his shirt. A few more feet and they came to the top of the hill and Angus pulled the trap to the side, the horses grateful for the respite. He reached in his pocket and gave them each a lump of sugar, patting them and easing their anxiety.

"I see what you mean about him handling the animals."

"Yes, those two ponies were his choice to purchase. They are quite beautiful, aren't they?"

"Yes they are. Angus must spend considerable time grooming them. Their black coats are immaculate! And I see he allows their manes and tails to grow out where many trim them. It is most becoming on them."

"Yes he does. He was particularly fond of this breed being they are from his home range. He talked Winston into purchasing them and we have never regretted that. They are Fell ponies, true mountain ponies from the Pennine Hills. They tend to show a wild side on occasion when put to pasture but once harnessed, they are a most friendly and willing pony, anxious only to please, especially to Angus. Daniel could do anything with these two. But then he is a great lover of animals also."

Watson looked about. The steepness of the hill had not prepared him for the view that lay beyond. From this vantage, one could see for miles in three directions. Off to the right, to the east, where the forest had been cut back for the plow were fields of wheat and hay already several feet high blowing gracefully like delicate strands of fine threaded gold in the breeze. Rock fence separated field from pasture where cattle and horse grazed together. And beyond was the dark blue of the ocean that merged with the rugged cliff tops that bordered the edge of the pastures.

Off to his left, to the west, were more fields but these were separated into various sizes housing small cottages and farms. Men and women as well as children could be seen in the fields with shovels and hoes, weeding and watering the acres of vegetables that would be sold at market as well as preserved to sustain them through the cold weather months. Several of the field workers looked up and saw the trap stopped on the road. Catching Dorthea's attention, they waved then turned back to their labor.

Directly ahead, Watson had saved the manor for last. Far in the distance stood the four storied gray building that had frightened Dorthea that first day of her arrival. Gone was the drab gray of the stone. Gone were the neglected gardens and paths. Instead what Watson looked upon was an elegantly restored light gray manor house with an awe inspiring entrance of emerald lawns amid a profusion of colors. A long drive of light colored rock led to the entrance and was complimented on both sides with rows of green low cut shrubs. "This is unbelievable!" Watson exclaimed.

"Quite different from my first impression isn't it?" Dorthea smiled at him.

"I must say that if I had seen the manor as it is now and then heard your tale I would most likely have doubted you. And I mean no offense by that."

"None taken, John. Every time I arrive at the crest of this hill I have Angus stop the trap so I can look upon the beauty that Winston has created. There are times that I can hardly believe my first impression of the place myself. Yet, despite its beauty and grandeur now, it still holds that foreboding atmosphere; sometimes it is as if there is someone watching me. It does tend to unsettle one."

"Well, I will tell you this. Once Sherlock Holmes arrives, he will put this whole incident to right and you can be sure he will ferret out every little bit of evidence and logically explain all that is happening. And there is a logical explanation, Dorthea, trust me. Trust Holmes."

And me? He thought to himself. Who do I trust, for I, too, feel the same as Dorthea; that there is something wrong with this place, that there is the unmistakable and overwhelming skin crawling sensation that there are eyes watching. Are there really ghosts? Is Gray Manor haunted? If so by what and why? He hoped he sounded convincing to Dorthea but it was becoming difficult to convince himself that it was all imagination.

"I will try."

"Are you ready to go, my Lady?" Angus asked.

"Yes, Angus, let us return."

Angus mounted the trap and with a gentle tap of the reins on the rumps of Phillip and Emma, they set off once more for Gray Manor. Drawing nearer, Watson once again shook his head at the marvelous creations that Winston had instituted. "I can only say this is marvelous, Dorthea," he said when the trap pulled lazily to a stop.

"Yes it is, and later I will show you our very own maze. Winston had the shrubs planted when they were small, for Daniel you see. Over the years, as Daniel grew, Winston allowed the shrubs to grow. They are over five feet tall now and we always have such fun….." she bit her lip and looked away.

"Come my dear, let us freshen up, eat a quick bite and have a lie down until dinner. Things will appear much brighter once we have removed some of this travel fatigue."

"You are correct, John."

"Oh look," Watson said. The butler and several of the maids as well as the cooks filed out of the front doors. "They must have seen us coming."

"Yes, they have someone watching , for they feel it is their duty to greet me upon my return from a journey. At first I was rather embarrassed by it all but now it reminds me that they do think of me and it is rather reassuring. It has become a much happier place since Winston's father died."

"My Lady," the butler strode forward to help Dorthea from the trap.

"Thank you Conway. John, this is Conway, my butler. And this is Justine my cook, Gwinn the kitchen maid, Merryn, Justine's daughter and my lady's maid and this is Anne the house maid. We keep a simple staff here and if and when an occasion arises where we need help, we hire from the village. This is my dear friend, John Watson from London. He will be visiting for some time."

"I will see to the bags, my Lady," Angus said.

"I will show Mr. Watson his quarters," Conway said.

"And I will get back to my kitchen. It is good to have you back my Lady," said Justine. "Well?" Justine nudged Gwinn.

"I'm coming, too," Gwinn said.

"Oh, Justine, could you have trays made up and send them to our quarters? We have not eaten since morning."

"Very good, my Lady."

"This way, sir?" Conway ushered Watson inside. They entered into a magnificent hallway that spanned more than thirty feet from left to right. The floor was of black and white marble and set down in a diamond pattern. Stairs of highly polished oak off set with a balustrade of dark oak curved from the hall upwards to the second floor landing and beyond. A massive chandelier of sparkling chrystal hung from the ceiling and along the walls were portraits of the former occupants of Gray Manor.

Directly ahead, Watson saw the downstairs parlor, small yet comfortable enough for entertaining a few personal friends. To the right of that was a locked door presumably the hall that led to the sealed off east wing. To his left was a set of large pocket doors that led into the main drawing room. From there the room circled to meet at the large opened glass doors of the solarium.

"This way, Mr. Watson," Conway urged.

"Yes, yes of course. I must say, Dorthea, this is marvelously done!"

"Yes, it is. Most of it simply required a good old fashioned cleaning, but Winston did have the walls repapered and the ceilings repainted. He has such an eye for design." They followed Conway up the stairs followed closely by Angus with their bags and Merryn. "Give Watson the King's room would you Conway?"

"Yes my Lady. This way, sir."

"I will see you for dinner? We eat at seven sharp. My room is two doors down from yours, on the left."

"I suggest you eat and lie down, my dear. You do look done in from all the travel," Watson said.

"I will, John. I am rather tired."

Watson hesitated in the hall and watched as Merryn gently guided Dorthea to her room. She'd tucked her arm into Dorthea's and their two heads were close, speaking softly together. Dorthea looked exhausted and he feared now that they had returned, her earlier imaginings of hauntings and ghosts would return.

"Sir?"

"Oh, thank you Conway. I simply wished to make sure Dor...Lady Pearl was all right."

"As do we all, sir." Conway set Watson's bags on the trunk at the foot of the bed. "Shall I see to your things, sir?"

"No, thank you, I can manage."

"Very good, sir. Is there anything further?"

"No, thank you once again." Conway nodded and closed the door quietly behind him.

Chapter Five

Watson sighed wearily and sat on the bed aware now how exhausting the coach ride had been. He eyed his bag on the trunk, heaved another sigh and decided to unpack later. He looked about his room. It was a very large room, the wood of the floor freshly polished, a length of rug between the two chairs that faced the fire place; a small table with several books nearby. The four poster bed commanded the room with nightstands and a large wardrobe of the same reddish brown mahogany. There were two sets of mullioned doors and Watson saw that he was in a corner room.

He drew the doors open and a fresh breeze swept about the room as he stepped onto the balcony. It was a narrow bay style that extended from the building five feet. A single chair and table rested here and he looked at it longingly, knowing if he sat now, he would not get up.

But the view was spectacular. He gazed out across the pastured fields to the west. Several head of cattle were contentedly grazing, their tails briskly swishing back and forth to ward off the insects. Beyond lay the moors blanketed in dark green moss, an occasional stand of birch here and there. A sliver of blue twisted and curved between the hills and rocks, a narrow stream, quiet and lazy meandering its way through the moors loosing itself behind an outcrop of rock.

He went to the other set of doors and again stepped onto the balcony there. From here the entire northern exposure of the estate was spread out before him and there was the maze Dorthea spoke of. He traced its course where it twisted and turned, sharp and abrupt, came to a dead end, twisted again over and over until after some time, he was able to determine the route that would lead him out. To the left and right of the maze were tall cedars that hovered like guarding sentries and beyond was a low rock wall that edged the back of the maze.

Beyond the wall was an untamed cluster of trees where a footpath could be seen cutting through. There stood the Gray Mausoleum, the roof of the marble enclosure could be seen on the knoll where it was built. He could almost make out the now righted statue that had injured Winston in his first accident.

Was it an accident? Was the staircase an accident? Was the fishing outing with Daniel an accident? Too coincidental all three accidents would happen to Winston. But as Holmes always stated, there's no such thing as a coincidence.

A knock on the door brought him about and Anne entered with his tray. Smelling the warmed bread and the steaming soup, Watson's stomach rumbled. He checked his timepiece and saw that it was nearly half past three. He ate quietly then, sipping the last of the tea near the window, he stared out into the maze once more and wondered how long Holmes would be.

Dorthea was exhausted from the journey, more so than she had imagined. But at the first moment she set foot back into the manor, that feeling of fear began to creep back into her. She shivered and tucked her arm into Merryn's and allowed her to lead the way to her room.

The room was gloomy and chilly and the overcast sky lent very little to dispel her fears, but Merryn's chatter kept the forced smile upon her lips. She picked at the food on her tray and finally sent it away barely touched. Alone at last she did what she had done so many times the past several months.

The drawer of the nightstand opened, the photographs of Winston and Daniel came out. She sat for some time in the chair near the window holding them to her, tears falling silently down her face waiting for the inevitable whispers that would come. Exhaustion taking over, the photographs slid to her lap. She lay her head back and finally slept.

A tap at the door brought Watson upright in the bed. He stared keenly about the room now saturated with a hazy gray hue that was alarming and frightening. A chill swept through bringing with it the ghostly specter of a white mist that sent the lace curtains floating about the window. His heart beat wildly. Strange noises, light tapping, swishing noises. Then he remembered, he'd forgotten to close the balcony doors and it was the lace curtains that blew about the room. He sighed with relief. Logical and rational, Holmes would have said.

The patter of a light rain in the dark beyond sent a chill through the room once more and he remembered he was at Gray Manor. How easy it was, he thought, for Dorthea to imagine seeing ghosts. Logical and rational.

Where the devil was Holmes? The tap once more. "Sir?" he heard Conway call.

"Yes, what is it?"

"Dinner in one hour, sir."

"Thank you, Conway." With his heart beat nearly normal, Watson rose and stretched then turned up the lamps. He had napped longer than intended and chastised himself. He planned on a short nap and a quick look about the grounds. He wanted to acquaint himself with the layout of the buildings as well as the rooms of the house so as to be able to inform Holmes upon his arrival. Once again, he hoped Holmes would arrive soon. He went to the opened doors and saw how dark it was outside and cursed the rain. He could barely make out the outline of the maze now, a blanket of darkness against the black of the path that twisted inside.

There was something mesmerizing about it and the longer he stared into the darkness, the more apprehensive he became. Sweat formed on his brow as a moment of terror seized his very soul. The darkness intensified and he had a horrible premonition of being lost, worse, hunted down like an animal, in such a labyrinth of twisting and unending terror.

And then his heart caught in his throat. It was there, a movement in the maze! A shadow? A ghost? He crept to the edge of the balcony, leaning precariously far over its rail, willing his eyes to adjust. Again, a movement, swift and dark. Something or someone was running through the maze! Watson flew back in his alarm, pressing against the wall behind him, and in a blink, it was gone.

He stood for some minutes watching and waiting, holding his breath until his lungs ached, afraid he'd been seen. Once the shadow was gone, he cursed himself for allowing that moment of darkness, that moment of fear to overpower any sense of reason and sanity that he held. He closed the doors and locked them, dressed and went down for dinner, but deep inside that moment of fear lingered. He could not shake the sense of a clear and real danger that existed at Gray Manor.

He entered the dining room to find Dorthea already there. Standing at the end of the room, she was talking to a man that Watson had not yet met. The man towered over her, standing more than six feet tall. He was well dressed and clean shaven and nodded as Dorthea spoke. "John, please do come in. I would like you to meet Mr. Upland, my estate manager I spoke of earlier. Mr. Upland, this is John Watson, a friend from London. He will be visiting for a while."

"Good to meet you, sir. I hope your stay here is agreeable." Arthur Upland shook Watson's hand vigorously. Watson took a keen measure of the man. He wore his long dark hair swept back and tied at the base of his neck. The dark eyes were fierce and penetrating, reminding him of Holmes' steely blue stare, and Watson could sense he was a very strong and determined man. Although very handsome, his swarthy features were marred by a scar that ran the length of the left side of his face from temple to jaw line.

"John has expressed an interest in Cadwith and perhaps an adventure or two into the coves and inlets?"

"It would be my pleasure, Lady Pearl. We'll make arrangements soon. If we have no further business? Then I will take my leave and leave you to your dinner. It was a pleasure, Mr. Watson."

"My pleasure indeed. I look forward to our adventure."

Dinner was quiet, just the two of them, and once the smell of roast mutton with steamed potatoes enveloped the room, Watson temporarily forgot about the shadow in the maze. Downing course after course, he pushed his plate to the side, finally sat back in his chair and patted his stomach. "I must admit, Dorthea, that was the finest meal I've eaten in months. Years!" he expounded with a wave of his arm.

"I am sure you exaggerate, John, but I will send your compliments to Justine. She will be pleased. And the raspberry tarts? I specifically requested them for you tonight."

"They were delicious! I must say it is difficult to determine which are the better, Justine's or Mrs. Hudson. They both have a fine flavor and delicate crust. Most delicious!"

"Then I am happy that you are well satisfied. Shall we retire to the drawing room? I do not mind if you smoke there. The smell of a good pipe tobacco is somehow soothing and relaxing," Dorthea said rising. "If I recall, it is still Shipps, is it not?"

"Wonderful memory. Allow me," Watson jumped to take command of her chair. "And I do believe I will have a smoke. Allow me a moment to return to my room and fetch my pipe."

He was reaching for his pipe and tobacco when he heard a noise. He looked about, not able to place its origin although it sounded like a large object or person moving about. It came from behind him and although he stared intently at the fireplace there, it seemed the noise was now gone.

"I have not used the room overly much these past several months," Dorthea said when Watson rejoined her in the drawing room. "Why don't we pull back the drapes and open the doors? The rain has stopped and it is such a beautifully evening. Would you prefer some fresh tea or something a bit stronger, John."

The drawing room was much larger than Watson had imagined. Much care had been taken with the room to make it a warm and comfortable place for the family to retire after the evening meal. There were several books lying on a nearby table, architectural fundamentals as far as Watson could read in the soft light. On the floor near the fireplace was a wooden toy train and a ball, and he could picture Winston Pearl studying drawings in the books while a young Daniel played near the hearth at his feet.

"Is anything the matter?" Dorthea asked.

"No not at all. I was admiring the room."

"Yes it is quite beautiful. Winston loves this room."

Watson winced inwardly. He noticed the recurring changes in Dorthea's speech. There were times she referred to Winston and Daniel in the past, but since their return the reference was now, the present. She perhaps did not realize she was doing it. Perhaps it was the pressure of returning to Gray Manor that saw her slipping back into the frenzied belief of ghosts and haunting. He shivered involuntarily when he'd thought the same thing earlier at the sight of the shadow. There was something strange going on in this house. Something or someone…..lurked.

He crossed the room and pulled open the doors and a breeze smelling of wet grass wafted throughout the room. "Yes, in answer to your question. I will have a spot of brandy if you don't mind? And you?" He strode to the decanters on a side table.

"Sherry, just a half glass, thank you."

"What a beautiful evening!" Watson exclaimed. "Even in this fading light everything looks so inviting. Why don't we sit outside. It seems a pity to waste such beauty."

"Winston and I would sit out here most evenings when the weather was fine. Daniel would join us before bedtime and…looking back I am happy for those times. This evening reminds me of such times."

"I am sorry, my dear, I did not mean to upset you," Watson said.

"Nonsense, John. I am happy you are here and that I am finally able to speak of such things with a trusted friend. I think it does me good to speak of them. To remember the good times, the happy times."

"It is as I said before. Winston and Daniel will always be here, Dorthea, in your heart and mind; and always in your soul. They will never be forgotten no matter the time that passes or the course of life you chose to take from now on."

"You are a comfort, John Watson. I can see that you have also suffered an unbearable grief. It is a shame that one must suffer the loss of a loved one before one can truly sympathize with others that have. Happiness abounds but sorrow knows no friend."

"That is terribly philosophical, my dear."

"Truly, it is. I have thought much about the events and people these several months. When there is happiness, there is always a crowd, a group of people laughing and sharing and enjoying come what may. But when a tragedy strikes, when a loved one is lost, no matter what the cause, it seems that the survivor stands alone. Do not misunderstand me, John. The people of the village were a great comfort to me for several weeks, indeed, including the local constable and my dear friend Dr. Farley. But one does notice after a period of time that the visits become less frequent, the understanding less tolerant."

"I fear you are correct for I have noticed that also. Friends and relatives are there for the moment, but tend to stay away in the long of it. It is as if they do not know what to say or how to comfort you for no matter how much time passes, one always needs comfort for the loss of a loved one never goes away. The pain merely subsides to a dull ache that only the survivor lives with constantly. One always needs that occasional remembrance, or a quick visit or simply to have the company to speak and remember. Life and death. Happiness and sorrow. There are two sides to every coin and the space between is so long and dark."

"And now who is philosophical?"

Watson smiled not only at Dorthea, but at himself. Rarely had he the time to reflect on his past, his friendship with Ambrose, his marriage to Mary and yet suddenly in the past week, he had pushed his memories to the limits of pain, to the warmth and comfort of the happiness and closeness that love and friendship bring. He'd forgotten those feelings, pushed them back, as far back as he could muster in his mind, not wanting to travel those paths again. Yet, here he was. The same paths; his friendship with Sherlock Holmes; his growing affection for Dorthea Pearl. Watson! He thought, you are a fool!

"And what do we have planned for tomorrow?" he asked.

"I thought I might show you around the grounds. Winston has done so much to improve the landscape. Daniel was always at his side. He even helped with the planting of the shrubs for the maze. I believe he has the proverbial green thumb where horticulture is concerned. He loves helping in the solarium. Many of the plants now thriving there were his to care for, although they have been neglected by me as of late."

"I would love to see them. I myself have no aptitude whatsoever for horticulture. All thumbs as they say."

"That is difficult to believe coming from a surgeon."

"Well it's true. Mending patients does not require the same profound dedication as plants. After all patients are, to some degree, responsible for themselves whereas plants are dependent upon so many variables least of which is mankind."

"And that is true to some degree. So all in all, you believe that in order for me to 'get better' as they say, that I am responsible for myself?"

"Come now....you have thrown that sentence into a whole realm of categorical discussion. There are underlying circumstances for the situation in which you have been thrust. Your situation is simply not one of mending broken bones or a physical ailment, such as congestion of the lungs. There is the apparent perception of sights and sounds that you have been experiencing that requires study and analysis to determine the validity of them."

"Do you think I am making this all up? That I am hallucinating? Losing my mind, John?" Dorthea cried.

"No! Of course not!" Watson sputtered, nearly spilling the contents of his glass. "Goodness knows it is not difficult to perceive the presence of something or someone when there are strange noises and shadows everywhere!"

Dorthea jumped up from the chair, spilling her glass. "You have seen them? Oh, John, tell me that is so!"

"I have seen shadows, Dorthea, in the maze and according to Holmes, if he *was* here, there would be a logical explanation for them. It was dark and I could not see very well."

"But you saw shadows. You saw them!" she cried.

"Yes, but please don't misconstrue what I have said, because there are many plausible explanations for shadows in a maze, outside, in the dark, in the rain. There are animals that may be roaming the premises. There are staff that may have been out for a walk. Many explanations, Dorthea. But see here, I am so very sorry I have brought attention to the matter."

"I am not, John, for it has given me hope."

"I don't wish it to be a false hope."

"Any hope is good hope, John. I can feel it in my heart. They are with me still."

Watson smiled outwardly at her face, the furrowed lines of pain and worry temporarily replaced with a hope that now brightened her features. Inside, he cursed. Why did that have to slip out? Why had he been so thoughtless? Perhaps because he himself had that niggling shadow of doubt that perhaps Dorthea was not wrong?

"You have lifted my heart and my spirits. I know now that I can count on you and Mr. Holmes to put this situation to right. I feel that I may be able to rest easy tonight and so I will be retiring, John, if you don't mind."

"Not at all, I shall see you to your room." Watson laid his pipe down and extended his arm and Dorthea tucked hers inside. They mounted the stairs, speaking in hushed voices, hers excited, his respectful, their steps barely heard on the carpeted floors. Merryn was in the hall already waiting for Dorthea.

"It was a beautiful evening was it not, my Lady?" Merryn nodded to Watson.

"Yes, Merryn, it was beautiful indeed. Goodnight John. I am very happy that you are here."

"As am I, Dorthea. Goodnight. Good evening, Merryn."

"Good night, Mr. Watson."

Chapter Six

He leaned against the door, sickened by his own thoughtlessness. What had he done? He was entrusted to help Dorthea, to accompany her to Gray Manor, to help her past her grief and her hallucinations of ghosts. But he had seen the shadows himself. Were they shadows of somebody real or had he truly seen ghosts in the maze? Were they really ghosts? Was there such a thing as a ghost? Was there such a thing as the soul of the dead that returned to haunt and torment the living? He did not know. Either way, he had hindered Dorthea's recuperation rather than helped. He set her back instead of guiding her forward. What a fool he was! He cursed under his breath and wished Sherlock Holmes was there. He would know how to handle the situation. He always did.

He pulled himself from self-recrimination and turned towards his quarters but remembered he left his pipe still smoldering on the tray. He returned to the drawing room where several lamps were still lit, the doors still open. He retrieved his pipe, closed the doors and turned out the lamps. He hesitated at the stairs for he was not tired and he was still too angry at himself to sleep. He returned to the veranda to think.

He sat and relit his pipe, enjoying the light breeze that brought the smell of fresh cut grasses and flowers to his nose. London had none of that, he thought. Only the smell of the city, of people bustling along the street, horses smelling of sweat and dried hay, and the ever present smell of the smoke from the factories.

He imagined what it would be like to live in such a place with servants and grand living quarters. Being able to purchase whatever one needed, or wanted, without a thought as to how that money was earned. Earned by others yet by law belonged to you. In some aspects he envied the rich, the manner in which they lived, but upon reflection, he was more than happy with his meager income. At least he had earned his pension through service in the military, through hard work and honesty. And now he continued to earn his way through his service with Sherlock Holmes. Almighty! But he wished Holmes would arrive soon.

His pipe spent, Watson rose and, closing the doors, went to the fireplace to tap out the remnants of the tobacco. The room was dark for he had already put out the lamps. Out of the corner of his eye he caught a movement in the shadows. Immediately the image in the maze came to mind and terror swept over him.

For a moment he held his breath until the rationality of Holmes came to mind. He crept silently around the furniture stopping near the door, and held back in its shadow. He watched and waited, for what, he did not know. After several minutes in the silence he found no reason for his vigilance. There was nothing. The noise was gone. Had he really heard a noise, or had he imagined it. With a sigh of relief, he tucked his pipe into his breast pocket and went to his room. The lamp was still burning low on his nightstand. He left it thus and went to stand at the windows. Stealing a long look out into the night, he saw nothing. No ghosts. No shadows. He turned and went to bed.

Several quiet days passed and Watson and Dorthea spent their time touring the remodeled rooms of the west wing and sipping tea on the front terrace. He kept their conversations light, speaking only of the estate, the remodeling, and insisted that Dorthea rest often. He saw with each day that passed that dark circles were beginning to appear beneath her brown eyes. She napped longer each day and complained more often than not of a headache. She retired early and yet woke each day unrefreshed.

He should never have mentioned the shadows he saw. It was entirely his fault that she had regressed and it pained him deeply. Each evening he would sit out on his balcony in the darkness waiting for the shadow, but it never came. He would lay awake on the bed listening for the noises of that first night, but they never sounded. After three days he had to admit to himself that what he saw and heard were the shadows of the night and the noises of an unfamiliar house moving and shifting with its own begotten life.

Today there was no getting around it. Dorthea must attend to matters of the estate. The morning was spent with Conrad going over the household accounts and the afternoon with Arthur Upland dealing with matters of the estate. Watson was left to his own devices. He spent some time in his room reading and writing down an account of the events thus far for Holmes should he ever arrive. He wandered about the lawns, drifting to the back where he walked through the gardens filled with herbs and vegetables, trees of apples and plums already abundant with small green fruits. He came to a stop at the maze, undecided whether to attempt its course alone, the terror of that first evening still tugging at his heart. He decided not to.

Dinner was rather quiet that evening. Dorthea seemed preoccupied throughout the meal and spoke very little. She set her glass down and sighed. It had been a long day going over the household accounts and the more urgent matters of the estate. "Is there anything the matter, Dorthea?" Watson asked. "You are terribly quiet tonight."

"No, but I think I will retire early tonight. I wanted to ask if you would like to take a walk about the hills and moors tomorrow? Mr. Upland assures me the weather will be fine and I feel as though I must get out. Dealing with all the estate affairs that Winston was so proficient at can be so exhausting."

"If you feel up to it tomorrow would be fine. I will be looking forward to it."

"Then on that note," Dorthea stood, "I will retire. I plan to read a little and then get plenty of rest. The walk about the grounds is a long one, so be sure you have good walking shoes ready. Good night then."

"Good night, Dorthea." He saw her to the door where Merryn was waiting, so he retired to the drawing room, poured a large brandy, lit his pipe and went to sit outside on the veranda. The evening was soft and warm with a gentle breeze that was relaxing and enjoyable. He sat for some time, even though he'd finished his brandy and the fire died in his pipe. The night grew darker, the stars brighter, the dipper now in full glow. He heard the mournful call of a night owl and then another as if the first were answered by its mate. He sighed heavily and went inside.

The drawing room was dark, the only light came from a lamp that remained lit in the entry. He was walking through when this time he absolutely distinctly heard muffled sounds. He froze and listened.

Yes, there it was; the unmistakable sound of feet, muted and nearly silent on the tiled floor. It had to be human. After all, ghosts don't make noises, do they? He followed the sound which led him down the hall and towards the solarium. Despite the darkness, the moon reflected through the windows to show him the source of the sounds. In front of him, stood Dorthea. She was in her nightdress. standing very still as though she had lost her way. Her long brown hair hung loose about her shoulders, and her feet were bare. The moon stretched across the room resting upon her with a pale ethereal glow, and Watson shivered.

"Dorthea? Dorthea, are you all right?"

But she did not answer. He laid a gentle hand on her shoulder, "Dorthea?"

She turned slowly, her face vacant and silent, her eyes glassy and void of any recognition. The warmth of Watson's hand seeped into the coldness of her skin and moments passed before any hint of recognition came to her eyes. "John, is that you? What are you doing here?" She looked about confused. "What am I doing here? How did I get here?"

"I heard a noise and followed you here. You do not remember coming here?"

"No, I do not. I heard voices, John, I heard voices calling me and somehow, here I came to be. What is happening, John. Why am I here?" Dorthea shivered.

Watson removed his jacket and placed it about her shoulders. "You must be sleep walking, my dear. That sometimes happens to people when they are overly distraught. I am sorry for our conversation at dinner. Somehow it must have upset you so that you were thinking of it even as you slept. Come. I will take you back to your room. You are shivering. And good lord no wonder, you have nothing on your feet on this cold stone!"

Dorthea allowed Watson's arms to envelope her and lead her to her room. He lit a small lamp on her dressing table and Dorthea wrapped the thick quilts about her to stop the shivering. "Are you all right now? Would you like me to fetch Merryn?" Watson asked.

"Yes, I am fine, but do not disturb Merryn. I cannot imagine what has come over me but I am relieved you were there once more to rescue me."

"Would you like me to stay, even for just a moment?"

"No thank you, but do please leave the lamp burning? I will feel safer with it on."

"Do you feel unsafe here, Dorthea?"

"No not unsafe as regards to my life. I only meant that the light would be there if I should happen to wake suddenly and reassure me as to where I am."

"I understand. Is there anything else I can do for you before I go?"

"No, but thank you so much for simply being here and being my friend."

"No thanks are necessary among friends." Watson kissed her on the cheek. "You rest now. I am just down the hall if you should call out and need me."

"Thank you but I will be all right. Good night, John."

"Good night, Dorthea."

Watson waited in the hall for a few moments, listening at the door. Dorthea must have been upset at their conversation earlier and it had been weighing on her even unto the depths of her unconscious as she slept. He chastised himself that he had allowed the conversation to go so far this early in the stages of her grief. He vowed to be more careful in the future.

Back in his room, he could not sleep and went to sit in the wicker chair on the balcony. The breeze was still warm and gentle, the moon and stars hazy behind a now beclouded sky. He could see the layout of the maze, the darkened shapes of the shrubs and the gray twisting paths of doom. What was it about that maze that terrified him so? He could not think of a basis for his fear nor conceive truthfully how the manifestation of fear of the place had entered his head. Yet it was there. It was so real it made his heart pound, it drew beads of sweat on his brow. But there were no shadows tonight. No ghosts. He went inside and went to bed.

The following morning he rose early. Not wishing to disturb the rest of the household, he went to sit outside where the calming sound of the water as it trickled down the rock in the fountain helped to ease his mind.

"This is a fine morning, is it not John?" Dorthea sat.

"Yes it is. I must have dozed for I did not hear you approach. But I was thinking that Holmes might even enjoy a day such as this," he exclaimed. "And how are you feeling this morning?"

"Much better thank you. Whatever it was that was on my mind last night seems to have completely cleared and I slept sound after. Thank you, Anne," she said to the maid who set a tray of tea and breakfast on the table. Have you eaten this morning?"

"Not yet. It was such a beautiful day I decided to step out and do some thinking. We do not have such weather in London. There the wind blows the black smoke of the factories about and the smell of horse and dung permeates the air. It is so fresh here. So vibrant and wonderful!"

"I guess I have taken that for granted as I very rarely visit the city. But here, we will eat and I have proposed a tour today."

"A tour?"

"Yes. Remember? Today we shall walk about the moors and perhaps we will have time to visit the cliffs as well. Winston and I did much of that while Daniel ran ahead of us and enjoyed being a boy. You know, rolling in the grass, climbing trees, all those things that young boys do. It will give me great pleasure to show the estate to you but it is best seen on foot. Are you up to that?"

"As up to as I can be, Dorthea. We will, of course, take it slow for I am not accustomed to walking all day at my age."

"Your age!" Dorthea scoffed. "Why you are not much older than I so stop that nonsense of age. I will have Justine pack us a bag lunch, because I wish to show you Gray Manor alone, selfish person that I am."

"Selfish, indeed." Watson smiled at her. "I will change into comfortable walking shoes and be down in what? Half hour?"

"Good," Dorthea smiled.

"We are going riding?" Watson asked when Dorthea met him near the pool in her riding breeches and boots.

"No, but I have found it to be much easier to traverse the moors and cliffs when not encumbered in the attire of the lady of the manor. Shall we?"

Watson hoisted the small backpack of food and water over his shoulders and they set off.

"We will make the loop going west to the Bennering Moor. It is most beautiful there John. So what shall we talk about?"

"Whatever you wish."

"About Ambrose? I feel now that you are here, somehow he is also."

Watson swallowed hard. The change in Dorthea this morning was terribly drastic from that of her demeanor over the past several days. Her spirits were high, her face refreshed and cheerful not unlike Holmes after a dose of his seven percent solution. He gave her a searching look and wondered. The conversation had quickly turned to subjects he did not wish to speak of but he knew in his heart that he must. He knew that Dorthea must. They had both suffered the loss of Ambrose and had each suffered in their own way, silently and apart and he knew it was time for their loss to be shared as it should have been all those years ago. "He was my good and dear friend, Dorthea. I am only sorry there was not much more I could do for him."

"I have thought of that day often and know in my heart that you did what could be done. It is not you I blame, John. It is the man who fired the shot. What a waste of life."

"Two lives actually. The celebration was going along very well until the argument started. And I do not remember what it was about, even."

"Nor I, but I'm sure it was over something to do with the mine, of course. It always was. There was always that feud over who dug the deepest tunnel, or who found the

richest vein or some such silly nonsense. But you know
how men get when the drink has been too much."

"Yes, I have seen it time after time."

"I think of him nearly every day, and even more so
now that I am alone. But I am happy that we have had an
opportunity to speak of him. He was and still is so very
dear to me. I only wish that Daniel had the opportunity to
know him. He is much like Ambrose, you know. Daring
and dashing. Full of….."

"I think of him often, also. And I miss him very
much," Watson replied quickly.

"Ah, here you must be cautious," Dorthea blinked
tears away. "The wind blows wickedly here, sometimes
so strong it tends to bowl one over!" They had crossed
the fields and were climbing steadily when they were
struck by a blast of wind. They stepped onto the rock that
began their ascent up the tor. Watson was relieved that the
conversation had changed. It was becoming much too
painful and he did not want to be responsible for any
more sleepwalking on Dorthea's part.

"I can see that," he laughed hanging on tight to his
hat. "Once we clear the pastures here the wind becomes a
sweeping hand."

Dorthea laughed and drew her hat about her head, the
long ties whipping backwards in the wind. "It is
wonderful isn't it?" she called over the wind. "We are
approaching Bennering Moor but first we must cross the
Devil's Tor. It is so called because the legend is that the
devil came to the Tor one fine summer in search of a fair
maiden. He was tricked by the townspeople into believing
that a fair maiden would meet him here. He waited, but of
course she never came. The townspeople went deep into
the caves and hid from him. He grew so angry he called

up the rocks to rise from the ocean and blocked all the entrances to the caves. The rocks grew and grew until they became huge cliffs, contorted into all shapes and folded upon themselves leaving this massive outcrop of rock which then merges with the moor."

"That is some legend. What happened to all the people in the cave?"

"Most died according to the legend. Those that survived still live in Cadwith. Come, I will show you our favorite spot! Be careful when crossing this expanse of granite, it can be slippery in places and it rises continually until we reach the summit. You see those large stones? Granite posts to mark the way. It is said if you step off the path from between the posts, you will be lost forever in the sinking wetlands that surround all these small hills leading up to the great Devil's Tor."

"But it is as dry as a bone here."

"Now perhaps, but once the raining season is upon us, beware of where you step. The moors fill with small pools and sink holes and it becomes treacherous to be out on them. Especially after dark when one cannot see the way."

"And you know so much of this, how?"

"Winston, of course. You forget he grew up here. Later when Lord Pearl died, Winston became his old self once more. Although he never did speak to me of the horrendous nightmares that haunted his dreams he did introduce me to the moors and cliffs. I fell in love with the place immediately. And he did truly love this place, and when Daniel and I would accompany him here, he would tell us tales of his adventures through the moors. I think he named each of these rocks and he would tell us a tale of the Circle of Stones which lies there, just below the summit. Hurry! We are nearly there!" Dorthea pushed forward and shouted, "I will race you to the top!"

"Not fair!" Watson shouted from behind. "I have the weight of the pack and the disadvantage of ignorance of the landscape!" But Dorthea only laughed and raced forward. Out of breath she waited for him at the top. Watson arrived out of breath, dropping the pack and gripping his knees with his hands, bent over trying to catch his breath.

"Breathtaking isn't it?" Dorthea cried.

"Allow me to first catch my breath before you take it away once again," Watson said. He turned to view the expanse before him and sat atop the summit, his knees tucked to his chest. "Absolutely breathtaking, Dorthea. I must admit this was well worth the agonizing climb up here."

"It is our favorite spot, John. Look there. You can see where the water pools are filled with moss and carpeted with wild flowers. At this distance, even the thick gorse looks beautiful when blended with the lavender of the heather. It is so peaceful here with only the wind at your back and the beauty before you."

"Yes it is but for the climb."

Dorthea drew closer and said, "It isn't so bad, John, once you get used to it. Look there, that is the Circle of Stones of which I spoke. Winston told Daniel and I that it is as old as the Cornish coast itself, perhaps older. The stones are all of irregular shape yet all lean and tall and arranged in a circle. He suspected the stones to be of granite because there is that trace of mica in them which gives them a diamond glint when the sun shines. He thinks they were erected there by the old gods. The local people would make pilgrimages here to pay them worship. The table in the center, there you can just see it from this angle, has been broken in two. The legend is that there were sacrifices held on that table and the final sacrifice was a blasphemous person. When she was sacrificed, the granite slab was broken. It was a bad omen to those who lived here and the Circle of Stones had been rendered unusable. Apparently after the slab was broken, no one ever came or made pilgrimages here again."

"That is a gruesome tale. Where do you suppose he came up with that?"

"From the old villagers and country folk that once lived on this moor. It seems to be pretty much uninhabitable, yet there are those people that managed to make a living here. Raising some cattle, mostly sheep and if you look off in the distance, you can see them still roaming the moors. There are wild ponies, also. Daniel would have such fun with them. He would race after them pretending to be as free as they, running like the wind without a care in the world. But," she caught herself before the tears filled her eyes "....sheep are more adaptable to the rugged terrain here and are much more capable of sustaining a living from the short grasses that grow. Although, there is the occasional sheep or cow that ventures one step too far into the wetlands of the marshes and is never found again."

"I would suspect if the wetlands are that dangerous it must happen more than once that the errant human being is also lost to the moors."

"On occasion, but rare. The people who live here are very cautious on the moors. They have learned to respect the land and venture no further than the seasons dictate."

"You have become well versed regarding this land, Dorthea. I am profoundly impressed!" Watson declared.

"It is Winston. He always speaks of this place with such excitement and deep love. Once his father was no longer here to shadow his every move, Winston was once more that carefree and loving man that I had married. Look there," she pointed to the east. "It is far away, but you can see the entire layout of Gray Manor. Even from this distance, the work that Winston has done is discernable and beautiful."

"Yes it is, oh, I was not aware that the maze behind the house stretches into the woods there. I do not see an end to it."

"No, the woods beyond the mausoleum stretch clear to the cliffs. Some of them have even gone so far as to stretch themselves beyond the edges of the cliffs and appear to be hanging on only by their exposed roots."

"Look there!" Watson shouted and pointed below. "Far off, did you see? It looked like a person down there."

"That is possible. There are still people out here who love the moor and walk it daily, as well as those who tend the sheep crossing the next tor, over there. You see? There he is once again with his dog," she pointed.

"Yes, I see them now." Watson sat back, relieved that it proved to be a shepherd tending his flock. That feeling of being followed and worse, always watched was persistent and becoming somewhat alarming.

"Did you ever have a dog when you were growing up?"

"No, I would have liked, but my parents did not. Although now I do have my faithful bull pup."

"Daniel, also. He begs for a dog, something to keep him company when he plays. A companion. Oh, John. All those times he has looked at other children with their dogs playing on the moors, chasing sticks into the water and his eyes have yearned for such fun but he stopped asking for all those times we had refused. If I were to do it all over again, I would allow him as many dogs as he wished!"

"Dorthea, please don't....."

"I know, John." she had turned her face to hide the tears that threatened. Turning back, she said,"There are so many small regrets that I have thought of over these past several months. I do not know why that of the dog stands out. Perhaps because now I see how happy it would have made Daniel. It was so selfish of me."

"We all can think of things that we should have done or should have said, but in the end of it, there is not much we can do about them, but move on else they will tear at our hearts and our very souls until we can bare it no longer. We must remind ourselves that we did the best we could with the time we had and realize that the decisions we made at the time were the right ones for that time."

"Perhaps you are right, John. I have not come to those terms, yet. But with your help and that of Mr. Holmes, I am hoping I will be able to soon. I apologize for everything but there are times I simply must voice what is in my head and my heart or I fear I will truly lose my mind. I have born these feelings alone for such a long time!"

"Do not fret on my account, Dorthea. I understand wholly. I...well truth be told, I do not like to see you so distressed. I feel so helpless that I am unable to help a dear friend..."

"Don't feel that way, for your presence here alone has been a help. And knowing your friendship is there to guide me should I need it is more than I can ask for. I am so grateful for that. And I know that you above all else understand the need to speak of lost ones, the need to remember the love and goodness and come to terms with the pain of their loss. It is the only way one can begin to move forward, perhaps. But there! I've wiped away the tears."

Dorthea stood and put out her hand to Watson. She pulled him up and said, "Are you ready for the walk back? We must be very careful on our descent. It slopes steeply in parts and tends to pull you forward. We can cross at the bottom of the summit and turn north where we can skirt the outside of that small thicket of birch there. The animals have paved a trail that we would also use and it leads, in a round-about fashion, to the cliffs far to the east."

"Quite a distance, but I am ready if you are," Watson smiled.

"Then let's have at it. If you think the moors are breathtaking, wait until you see the Camel Cliffs!"

Watson hoisted the packback onto his shoulders and said mostly under his breath, "I can hardly wait!"

They reached the base of the Devil's Tor and followed the trail between the rolling green mounds of the lesser tors. Heather and other low vegetation covered the ground here and the hoof prints of sheep were quite discernible in the dried soil. The sun rose steadily and beat down upon them, the wind a mere whisper between the rolling hills. Up ahead, Watson could see the stand of birch trees gradually getting closer and he proposed a short break. They crossed an open expanse and the wind drifted out of the trees stirring the leaves into a flutter. Finding a large rock to perch on, he lowered the pack and rubbed his shoulder.

"Is the pack that heavy, John?"

"No, it is just that every so often that old bullet wound begins to ache."

"I had forgotten of that. If you wish, I can carry the pack."

"Nonsense, Dorthea, I will be fine. I see there to the south you can see the roof of Gray Manor."

"Yes, you can see the building for some distance in all directions but the way to the north and east is obstructed partially by the forest."

"Yes, I can see that. We must have Holmes accompany us on this tour of the estate. I am sure he would find it most interesting."

"I can see that it is nearly noon and the rumbling of your stomach is like thunder. Perhaps we should lighten the pack of its contents and eat our lunch here? It is a beautiful spot and we can sit just there beneath that rock outcrop, out of the wind."

"Oh thank you." Watson set the pack down and rummaged through its contents. "What have we here? Ah, a jug of water, what every hiker must carry I suppose. Several apples and here, these are?"

"Pasties, John," Dorthea laughed and unwrapped the small dough filled pastry."

"Why, I have never seen the like!" Watson exclaimed.

"It is a staple food here in Cornwall, dating back several hundred years. It is pastry filled with chopped onions, potatoes, beef, turnip, or many times, whatever has been left in the pantry. They are spiced and are delicious. Justine is a wonder with these."

"They are still warm. Amazing. I shall have a go at it." Watson bit into the thick folded golden crust, into the potato, bits of onion and beef whose chunky texture filled the pallet. "Oh my! Oh my goodness. These are simply delicious!" he cried .

"I shall inform Justine you have said so," Dorthea laughed.

They ate their meal while the sounds of nature around them abounded. The wind blew lightly beneath the canopy of trees, their leaves rustling softly. Black redstarts with their orange under bellies flew above swooping back and forth searching for flies and other insects before returning to the contorted rock of the cliffs where they would continue their search of food in the tiny crustaceans of the beaches.   Swallows and warblers whistled, piercing the tranquility of the soft breeze while dozens of Mediterranean gulls screeched overhead, circling inland from the cliffs, their thick red bills a sharp contrast to the pale gray bodies.

"One would think it to be very quiet here in the country, but it appears not. There is an abundance of birds and buzzing insects."

"We are near Camel Cliffs. Most of these birds build their nests there. Some like the gulls, remain all year, but those like the redstarts migrate here and only come for the nesting season."

"Your knowledge of this area never ceases to amaze me."

"It is all due to Winston. As I said before, he loves it h...loved it here. And I have grown to share his feelings over the years. Now, without him, I do not know if I can go on. There are so many things here that remind me of him, remind me of our life together. A life I no longer have."

"Nonsense! You have many years left, my dear and although difficult as it seems now, you will get over this.

You must, if not for their sakes, but for your own. You have much to offer, Dorthea."

"Thank you. You always seem to know exactly the right things to say."

"It's simply that I have been through such a loss and know how the heart aches and the mind works. You must give it time. You'll see."

"Then we shall see. Are you ready to continue?" Dorthea folded the pasty wraps and tucked them and the water jug back into the pack. "The pack will be much lighter now. Here, munch this apple as we go. These are our very own grown, you know."

"Delicious. After you, my dear."

Dorthea led the way weaving through the stand of birch growing thick and tall. It was cool and somber here, the thickness of the trees muting the screeching of the birds, yet intensified the rustling of the leaves. Watson felt a sense of awe, a sense of reverence as though he had just set foot in a most holy and sacred place.

The woodland path, trampled over time by wildlife was narrow and weaved between the trees. It was grown thick with a lush green carpet of moss that flourished in the low light where shrubs and gorse could not, florescent as a backdrop to the scattering of wild primrose, violets and pinks. The redstarts and gulls flew ahead, screeching and circling, as though they themselves were drawing Dorthea and Watson towards the cliffs.

The soft padded moss underfoot soon gave way to rock, a smooth expanse of exposed granite. Ahead, Watson could see a threadlike beam of light compressed and slim against the crowded birch, but with each step that drew them nearer the cliffs and out of the trees the light increased, mushrooming as they approached the clearing ahead. Finally, stepping out into the open, the wind blew strong and toppled his hat from his head.

"You should have warned me about the wind here?" he shouted, stooping to retrieve his hat before the wind carried it over the edge.

Dorthea laughed. "I am sorry. It's just that I love that moment, that one very special moment when one steps from the quiet peace of the trees and into the buffeting of the strong wind. It is so exhilarating! I wanted you to experience that."

"I have and you are correct. It is most exhilarating!"

"Follow close now, John. We will circle just for a short walk here and you will see why this was our favorite place." Dorthea stepped carefully skirting the tree line which bordered precariously close to the edge of the cliff. This continued for some twenty feet before opening onto the summit, a broad flat area of granite of some fifty feet before it was taken over once more by the forest. She stopped and pointed and Watson was filled with wonder. The woods bordered the edge of the cliffs for miles, the cliffs themselves plummeting ruthlessly to the sea.

Pillar upon pillar of jagged rock struck out sharply and plunged sheer to the rocks and into the sea below. Gulls flew high, caught the wind drafts and soared towards the water, snapping fish in their beaks and turned, flapping with graceful ease against the wind to return to their young. The cliffs were filled with nests of the razorbills and guillemots that arrived and thrived on the lush and plentiful bounty provided by the sea. Along the cliff was a footpath that had been cut through the rock stretching from the top to the narrow strip of clear beach below.

"We are standing nearer the second hump of the Camel Cliffs so called as you can guess by their obvious resemblance to that of a camel. If you look there to your left is the first rise of cliff, a bit higher than this but much more jagged and treacherous. You can see how the cliffs plunge downward propelling the rocks into the sea creating something of a natural break from those crashing waves. Directly below us is the stretch of beach where Winston, Daniel and I would go for swimming and picnics. Right now we are standing in the center of the two cliffs, you can see the second there to your right. Not quite as high but just as treacherous. It follows the coast for some distance before it descends quickly in Cadwith. We have to approach the beach down there by using that path you see just there. It has been said that the path was worn by the pirates that would frequent this inlet." Dorthea pointed. "If we take the trail east from the house, it leads directly to that path and is much easier to descend. It is impossible from here."

"It is simply beautiful!" Watson exclaimed.

"Yes, Winston and I would come here, alone. This was our place. This was….well, you understand."

Watson put his arm about her shoulders and drew her close. She leaned into him and he said, "I do understand, Dorthea, indeed I do."

They stood for several minutes admiring the cliffs and the beach below. Far to the left the waves rolled in one after the other, smashing against the rocks spewing water and white froth into the air. A narrow outcrop of rock stretched into the water, seizing the hurling waves confining them to the sea. Within was the beach, quiet and serene in its own presence as though unaware of the dangers that threatened beyond the rock. Looking out upon the beach, Watson realized that that was the last place where Winston and Daniel had last been alive.

Chapter Seven

The return to Gray Manor was quiet, subdued as both were lost in their own thoughts. She thinking of Winston and Daniel, their picnics at the beach, Daniel laughing as he ran back and forth in the water. Her time alone with Winston and the romantic afternoons they lay in each other's arms at the summit.

Watson was thinking of Mary and his love for her, their time together and the hopelessness of life once she had gone. He cast a wary look more than once at Dorthea, sorry for her loss, concerned over her well-being and wished more than ever he could rid her of the pain that haunted her.

When they reached the manor, Dorthea excused herself to retire for the evening, requesting a tray be sent to her room. Watson walked her to her room. She saw the concern that furrowed his brow. "I am all right, John. I had such a lovely day and I apologize for my early retirement, but I hope you will forgive me."

He kissed her hand gently. "There is nothing to forgive. I myself am weary but I wish you to know that I had a marvelous time today. I only regret that there were memories that were brought to surface that may have upset you."

"There were some, but I am glad to speak of Winston and Daniel. They are, after all, my life. I will rest now. Here is Merryn. Good night, John."

"Good night, Dorthea."

"You look done in, my lady," Merryn said putting her arm about Dorthea's shoulder. "Let me draw you a nice warm bath."

Watson retreated to his room cursing himself for allowing things to have gone so far so soon. It was supposed to be a nice quiet day, a walk around the estate. But what had happened? Memories of Ambrose and Mary kept creeping through his brain, and Dorthea rambled with the constant mention of Winston and Daniel as though they were waiting just around the corner. He cursed himself for his feelings and he went to stand at the window. Dusk was already upon them and he picked at the meal now growing cold on the tray. He cursed again, this time at Holmes' absence. What on earth could be keeping the man?

He was on edge now, despite his fatigue. Pacing back and forth he threw his door open and retraced his steps down the hall. He lingered outside of Dorthea's bedroom, his hand poised to knock, but did not. His affection for Dorthea Pearl was as a friend only and to that end must always be. He intended to return to his own room, but decided to go down to the library. Perhaps a good book, he thought.

Merryn had turned down the lights and withdrew, leaving Dorthea, who pretended to be sleeping beneath her blankets. The hot bath and warm milk with her evening meal had made her drowsy. Yet despite her tiredness she rose and went to the large wardrobe in the corner of the room and pulled the doors open. Winston's clothes still hung there, his hats on the nook, his shirts side by side, his shoes beneath. She leaned into the shirts, pressing her face into them, drawing in the smell of his soap, of his sweat, of the very essence of his body, while her own shook with silent sobs. Tears that should have been gone long ago poured out and she sank to the floor clutching his clothes to her.

Her tears finally spent, she rose stiffly taking a shirt with her and took out her photographs of Winston and Daniel from the bureau drawer. Lying them beside her she crawled beneath the blankets once more. She traced Winston's face, Daniel's unruly hair. "I was at the summit today, my dear and I knew you were near. I know it won't be long now. I can feel it. I will be with you soon." She tucked the photographs beneath her arm and her eyes closed.

Watson had gone to the second floor and was now standing before the library door deep in thought. Dorthea had not shown him the library and he realized that it was probably the room that held the most tragic memories for her, for it was there she first set eyes on Winston's father. It was there she felt the darkness, the impression of an evil that lurked in the shadows, that lived in that library. Here was the beginning of the end of happiness for her and her family, although no one had seen it coming. Angrily, he pushed the door open. Darkness encompassed every corner but for a meager fragment of light straining through the filmed windows on the upper level. He saw a lamp on the desk and once lit, he went about the room lighting several more.

It was an enormous room filled with shelves and books. Above him was an upper level, a half floor that encircled the room, the shelves there full to overflowing with more books. There were books stacked on the floor, books on all the tables, books near the door and some by the fireplace. In the space between the books was wedged a large desk which was situated towards one end of the room with an enormous fireplace at its back. More books and papers were stacked high on the desk and surrounding chairs. Spread out across the top of the entire mess were pages of architectural plans that were held at each corner with more books. Peering at the blue prints, Watson could see that it was a plan of the west wing, the wing currently occupied, and that notes and papers of ideas had been hastily written and scattered about.

He lifted the top page and beneath was that of the Gray Mausoleum. The next page was of landscaping ideas for the gardens. He let the pages fall, picked up the lamp and strolled about the room. He glanced at the books, thick leather volumes of history, science and mathematics; volumes thick with dust and the smell of having never been opened. A noise, muffled and distant caused him to pause and listen, but it came no more. He continued his perusal of books when it happened again. Once more he stopped and listened and once more it was gone. He continued and came at last to where the spiral staircase stood and he went up. Holding the lamp here, he saw this was where the Gray family kept their easy reading. Volumes of Shakespeare, Chaucer, Keats, Shelley and more, lined the shelves. No dust here. Obviously the books here warranted better reading than those below. In the center of the half floor was a reading nook with a large window with padded window seats of fine burgundy wool on each side.

He set the lamp down and looked out the window and saw that he was facing the same direction as that of his bedroom upstairs and if he craned his neck, could make out the shadows of the tall cedars there. To his left the corner of the front of the building jutted out perhaps four or five feet obstructing his view to the front of the house.

Outside, a quarter moon, circled by an iridescent silver corona, hung in the sky. It cast a muted light about the objects below and once his eyes adjusted to the darkness, he could see more clearly the stand of cedars. A bird flew past the window and he jumped back, then laughed at himself at his foolishness. It perched on the protruding ledge, an owl, stopping for a moment with its prey in its claws before taking flight once more to its nest. He was about to fetch the lamp when a moving shadow caught his attention. He quickly extinguished the lamp and stood still in the darkened room, peering below.

It crept forward slipping between the trunks of the cedars and Watson followed its every movement. "He's moving to the front of the house, damn it all!" he whispered to himself, for now he knew it was no ghost.

Quickly he made his way down the stairs. There was a set of doors on the southern exposure of the solarium and Watson quickly went there. He tried to open them but they were locked tight. For several moments he watched, craning his head, his face pressed tight to the glass and soon he saw the shadow creeping from around the corner. He patted his pocket relieved his revolver was there. The figure froze momentarily, then with startling swiftness began to run towards the front of the house.

Watson looked in the direction he was running and saw the figure of a man standing there. He was waving his arms to someone…then he saw the ghost!

She appeared out of nowhere, white and ethereal, drifting across the shadowed lawn. The wind tugged at her nightdress and blew her hair in her face and she stumbled several steps before catching her balance.

"Dorthea!" Watson shouted into the glass, his fists beating against the handles that would not open. Alarm rose when he saw the shadow figure advancing, now shouting at the man at the fountain. The man at the fountain had seized Dorthea, drawing her over the rim and into the water of the fountain.

Pulling the gun from his pocket, Watson ran from the room. He threw open the front door and rushed into the night in time to see the shadow to his right fast approaching. He turned towards him, fearing he was the source threatening Dorthea and must be stopped at all costs.

Nearly upon him, the man shouted, "Watson, quick, stop that man!" Watson turned at the voice to see the man at the fountain with his hands at Dorthea's throat and plunging her headlong into the fountain forcing her beneath the water. He changed direction, running toward them now and although he knew his aim was not true, he fired one shot in the air. The man jumped as the shot rang out, thrust Dorthea from him, jumped from the pool and bolted across the lawn. He skidded on the wet grass, his arms flailing to catch his balance and Watson fired another round, this time aiming at the intruder. The bullet caught him and the man tumbled head over heels but instantly scrambled to his feet and fled behind the house.

"Holmes!" Watson shouted. "I'll get Dorthea!" Holmes sprinted past and Watson threw his revolver into the air. Catching the weapon, Sherlock Holmes sped after the retreating figure. He arrived at the back of the house in time to see the man disappear into the maze and out of sight. Holmes followed him, stopping several feet into the thick hedges and stopped to listen. There was nothing. No sound of feet, no heavy breathing. The man was indeed gone. He returned and found Watson bending over Dorthea Pearl.

The shots had awakened the servants who now emerged from the house, the lawn now well lit with lanterns. "Quickly!" Watson was shouting. "We must get her to bed and in some dry clothes!"

Angus came across the lawn, pushing everyone out of his way. "I'll take her. Step back!" he shouted. "I'll take her." He scooped Dorthea into his arms and Merryn quickly threw a blanket about them. He went carefully but quickly up the stairs and laid her gently on her bed.

"Now go, all of you. Gwinn and I will see to Lady Pearl. When we have set her in warm clothes, we will let you know. Now out!" Merryn ordered.

"Merryn!" Watson said from the doorway. "I am a doctor. I will examine her once you are done."

Merryn nodded shouting to Angus to fetch some hot water. The servants ran about the house, building fires, fetching more wood, fetching warm blankets. Inside Gwinn and Merryn quickly changed her into a fresh gown warmed by the fire.

Watson paced the hall outside Dorthea's door shivering himself, his wet clothes dripping to the floor. "Where were you, Holmes? It was a stroke of luck that you were about," he said through chattering teeth.

"Not luck, Watson. I have been about since that first day you left London. I have been looking into several things. Tonight I was mapping out the layout of the maze in relation to the rest of the grounds when I saw a figure emerge and go round back of the house. The moon was in his favor, I'm afraid, and he soon disappeared into the shadows. So I waited. I saw the lights go on in the library and soon saw you in the window."

"So it was you I was watching from the window?"

"Yes. I felt that by going to the front I might be able to see where he had gone off to or perhaps even discover his identity. But as I approached I saw him standing near the fountain and it was then Lady Pearl appeared. I knew immediately she was in danger and I shouted to warn her but she appeared not to hear me. It is you who should be commended, Watson."

"Not I surely, Holmes. I would not have been aware of anything going on at the front of the house if I had not seen your shadow, and thinking you to be the intruder, felt it my duty to stop you. It was only after your shout that Dorthea's danger became eminent."

"I think it would be best if you were to get out of those wet clothes also, Watson. It may be several minutes yet before Lady Pearl is up to your examination."

"Yes you are right. You will wait here, won't you?"

"I will not leave this spot. Go, before you catch your death."

Watson nodded. In his room he quickly changed, dressing quickly for the fire in his room had died to coals and the chill set his teeth to chattering once more.

"You could have taken more time, Watson," Holmes said when he appeared only a few minutes later with his valise. "They are still inside. It has quieted down and I am of the mind that they will be out soon saying she is finally resting. I've sent the young man, Angus, to dress and return. We will need him to stand watch at her door tonight."

Finally, Gwinn stepped out. "Lady Pearl is resting, and Merryn has asked you to go in, Dr. Watson, and she wanted me to tell you that Lord Pearl's clothes and photographs were on the bed when we entered."

"Thank you, Gwinn." Watson cast Holmes a wary glance and went in. The lamps were turned low and Merryn waited at the foot of the bed, her face anxious about her mistress. Gently he put his hand to Dorthea's forehead and brushed the hair from her face. Her eyes opened slowly

"How are you feeling, my dear?"

"I....I do not know what happened, John."

"First allow me to examine you. You have had a terrible turn and here I see a bruise upon your forehead. Is there anywhere else that pains you?"

"No, only my head hurts and my throat a little."

Watson looked closely and saw dark bruises forming about the delicate white of her skin "He has tried to choke you, my dear. You will have bruises for several weeks and your throat will be sore but you will be all right. That bump on your head should have a cool compress to take down the swelling."

"I will fetch a cloth and some fresh cold water," Merryn said. She left and Sherlock Holmes entered.

"I hope you are well, Lady Pearl?"

"Mr. Holmes! I am happy to see you!" she cried and attempted to rise but Watson insisted she lie still. "No, John, please allow me to sit. I must tell you what I can. What I remember. It was the strangest thing."

"If you feel up to it."

"I am afraid I must if we are to come to an end to this situation."

"If you feel ready, Lady Pearl," Holmes said.

"Well, John and I were out all day about the estate and I was so exhausted. I retired early. Once Merryn left I could not sleep. I rose and....and..."

"We know. Merryn found the clothes and photographs on the bed. We understand, Lady Pearl. Please go on," Holmes urged.

"I remember lying on the bed with my....items and ...and looking at them.....and I thought I was sleeping but I don't think I was...I saw..."

Chapter Eight

Winston stared up at her with loving eyes and the sweet smile that was always ready for her each day. She traced his face on the glass, his eyes, his nose, his chin and his lips. Drawing the photograph to her, she kissed those lips and hugged the picture close to her heart, closing her eyes. The sound of his voice came to her ears, the laughter they once knew, the small petty disagreements they had soon forgotten in their love making. Tears spilled and dropped silently to the bed sheets below and Dorthea rocked back and forth listening to the sound of his voice.

"Dorthea! Dorthea!" the voice called softly through the darkness of her half-conscious state. "Dorthea, my love, I am here. It is Winston, my love, here waiting for you!"

"I know my dear Winston for I can feel you still with me. I can feel your breath, your lips upon mine, the beating of your heart as we lie together. Winston, my dear husband where are you? Why cannot I find you?"

"Dorthea, I am here. I am waiting for you at the fountain. Remember the fountain, Dorthea? Remember the times with Daniel playing in the water? Remember our love, Dorthea. Come to me, my love. Come to me. I am waiting for you at the fountain."

In that waking few moments between sleep and consciousness, Dorthea rocked on the bed, holding tight to the photograph of Winston. The voice that whispered into the darkness was soft and inviting. Winston's voice. Yes, it was Winston's voice! She looked about the dimly lit room with a panic that tore at her very soul. "Winston! Where are you my dear! I am here. I will come. I will come." She dropped the picture to the bed and reached for the door.

"Dorthea, do not go by way of the solarium," Winston's voice whispered once more. "You must use the front entrance. The moon shines there and will give you light."

"Yes…yes…I will go there. I will be with you soon, my love. I will be with you and Daniel soon," Dorthea cried into the room. She threw the door open and looked about the halls. Finding it empty, her bare feet thudding softly as she ran down the hall, down the stairs and across the foyer.

She pulled open the entry door, the yellow of the moon shone bright here, reflecting off the glass walls of the solarium. The stone outside was cool to her feet but Dorthea did not seem to notice. She padded quickly outside. She saw him then. The figure of a man standing near the fountain. He caught sight of her when she started across the lawn and he held out his arms, whispering, "Dorthea, Dorthea my love. Come to me…..come to me and we shall be together always!"

"Winston!" Dorthea cried and her steps quickened. The wind blew her hair into her face and tangled her loosed night dress about her and she stumbled across the wet dew of the grass. Rising quickly, she was at last near and she cried once more, "Winston!"

She flung herself into his arms and they folded about her drawing her close. Crying into his shoulder she looked up into his face, into the face of her husband, dead now these four months. But how could he be dead? He was here, he was holding her, he was kissing her brow and she drew away and stared at Winston who was alive; or was it Winston?

The man drew back and a look of anger darkened his features. His hands went to her throat and tightened and he forced her down into the water. Dorthea fought, but his strength was no match for her. It was at that moment she heard shouting voices and the shot of a gun.

"I do not remember much else of what happened, Mr. Holmes," Dorthea said once done with her tale. "But I can tell you that I truly thought the man was Winston, that he was no apparition. But that cannot be, can it? But why would someone try to kill me, Mr. Holmes? Why?" she cried.

"That is exactly what we are going to find out, Lady Pearl. For now you must do something for me."

"Anything, I will do anything, Mr. Holmes."

"Your man, Angus was extremely shaken over this incident. The man will do anything for you even if it means death, although I do hope it will not come to that. I am posting him at your door for the night, only to be sure you remain in your room and remain safe, for him we can truly trust and count on to keep his watch. He will have orders to prevent you from leaving if you make an attempt and he will call out for help to stop you if need be."

"I understand fully."

"Good, now that that is settled," Watson said, "I will give you a sleeping draught and will leave you to get your rest. Angus will be outside your door and we will be just down the hall." Watson watched her drink the entire contents of the mixture.

She lay back on the pillows, her eyes drowsy and finally sleep overtook her. With a last look behind, Watson closed the door while Holmes instructed Angus of his charge. "And you," he said to Watson, "should take yourself to bed. You look exhausted, old man."

"Exhausted or not, I am sure sleep will evade me. But a good stiff brandy should help. Come. The library is one floor beneath us." Together they went into the library where Holmes found the cabinet of liquors and poured two drinks. Handing one to Watson, he took the other and went to sit in one of the chairs facing the desk. Watson drained his glass, poured another then went to sit in the chair opposite Holmes.

"I cannot think how fortunate it was that you were about, Holmes. Tonight might have had a far worse ending."

"Fortunate indeed, Watson. Tell me about what has been happening since you departed London."

"Not much. Things have been relatively quiet since we arrived here at Gray Manor. It rained for several days so Dorthea gave me a tour of the inside of the manor house. All the doors leading to the east wing are locked and we could not enter. I did not think to look for the keys she said Winston once had in his possession. Today we walked along the moors and up to the high tor and the Circle of Stones. From there we ate lunch and went round about the cliff tops where we had a most magnificent view of the beach below as well as the run of the coast line for miles."

"Was there...."

"I quite forgot. Several days ago, Dorthea had retired early and I was in the drawing room when I heard a noise several times but there was nothing. When I turned out the lights and was about to take my leave, I saw Dorthea walk into the solarium. She was in her night dress and when I approached her, it was as if she did not hear me or even recognize me. When she did come to her senses, she had no idea how she came to be in the solarium."

"Was there...."

"And I nearly forgot also, that when I was in the library this evening, I heard strange noises once more. A shuffling type of noise. It happened two, perhaps three times then I heard it no more."

"Can I speak now?"

"I am sorry, Holmes. It is simply that the thoughts are racing through my head and I am trying to remember all of them at once. Things come back to me quickly and if I don't mention them at that point, I am afraid I will forget them again. But yes," Watson indicated with a wave of his hand, "go ahead and speak."

"I was merely going to ask what you had made of that? Of the incident in the solarium?"

"I didn't know what to make of it, Holmes. I took it to be that she was merely sleep walking. It had not happened any other night....... until tonight."

"And that was nearly catastrophic, Watson."

"What do you make of it Holmes? What are we to do now?"

"What we have always done. Solve this case. That man at the fountain was no apparition, no ghost. Someone out there has set his mind to destroy every one of the Gray Manor bloodline and apparently has no conscience as to how he goes about it. And it must be someone who is very familiar with Gray Manor, its buildings, its outlay. He has an intimate knowledge of the maze for I saw him enter and in mere seconds there was no trace of him. How is he getting into the house is one question that must be answered. The other question is why?"

"I can tell you it does not appear to be any member of the staff here. From what I have gathered they all love and admire Dorthea."

"As in the fishing village of Cadwith, also. I have been making my way about, as you know I do, Watson, and asking questions. You are correct in that the people here admire her and her husband. I could not find a soul to say a word against them."

"Then perhaps it is not someone from their lives. Perhaps it is someone from the past, someone who has a deep seated grudge against James Pearl, the previous lord of the manor."

"If that is the case, we have more suspects than we care to. At the mention of his name, there was all manner of foul oaths and curses heaped upon his dead soul."

"Perhaps, it goes further back than that, Holmes."

"In what way?"

"I don't know. I truly do not know. I guess I am exhausted over the events and probably should get myself to bed." In the moment he mentioned it, he regretted it. How could he possibly convince Holmes about the tale of the sacrifices at the Circle of Stones? Could such a thing possibly be true? Did the Gray ancestors participate in such unearthly rituals? He didn't know. What he did know was that he wasn't about to explain and convince Holmes of such a thing. He downed the remainder of brandy and started for the door. "You know, I am much relieved you are here, Holmes. The responsibility of protecting Dorthea over these past several days has been daunting. I did not realize how much of a burden it was until I heard your voice shouting to me down there and a wave of relieve swept over me. Thank you for coming."

"You're welcome, Watson. Best get some rest. Tomorrow is another day. We will start fresh in the morning."

"Good night Holmes."

"Good night, Watson."

Chapter Nine

The next morning, Angus, still at his post, nodded to Watson when he went in to check on Dorthea. She lay asleep, looking peaceful, the lines of worry gone from her face. He put a finger to his lips when Merryn entered and whispered, "Do not disturb her, Merryn. She can use all the rest she can get. Just be here when she wakes."

"I will, Dr. Watson. It was a blessing you were here and a doctor besides. You saved our mistress's life. For that we all thank you, sir."

"It was not just I, Merryn, but Sherlock Holmes who was most instrumental. His quick wit and fast foot saved her and nearly caught the culprit."

"Whoever it is, Dr. Watson, we all hope you catch him, and catch him quick. The rope is much too good a punishment for that man. The nerve, trying to choke and drown our mistress."

"I will leave you to your vigil."

He sauntered down the stairs thinking of the events of last evening and wondered who really would want to kill everyone of Gray Manor. When he entered the dining area, Holmes was already there with Arthur Upland and Dr. Farley. Word had spread through the countryside into the village.

"She is sleeping and resting quietly, Dr. Farley," Watson said upon seeing him at the table. "I gave her a sleeping draught last night and she is doing well. Some minor bruising and a bump on the forehead, nothing more."

"Ah, I am relieved. Are you a doctor, Mr. Watson?" Farley eyed Watson.

"Yes, as a matter of fact I am. I am sure Dorthea did not wish everyone to know for fear they would approach me, but there was no need. I see the people of Cadwith are already in capable hands," Watson poured himself a cup of tea.

"She is well, then? Unharmed?" Upland said.

"Yes, she will be fine."

"Then I will not disturb her with estate business. The matter can wait for another day or two."

"I do not know if you have both met my friend and colleague, this is Sherlock Holmes from London. Holmes, this is Dorthea's estate manager Arthur Upland and Dr. Leonard Farley, the local doctor hereabouts."

"Sherlock Holmes?" Farley stole a look up and down at the man. "I have heard much of your reputation, Mr. Holmes. I was not aware that Lady Pearl was an acquaintance of yours."

"She is a dear and close friend to Dr. Watson here. She came to me on Watson's insistence and fortunately it was well grounded insistence. The man who assaulted Lady Pearl last night was not an apparition, nor a ghost. There is a real danger to her person and finally it has come to light. No more pushing aside her talk of spirits or placating her rantings as a woman grieving a loss. The danger here is real. Do either of you have any idea or can you think of anyone who would wish the lady harm?"

"I cannot," Upland said. "I have lived in Cadwith all my life, having been born and raised here. I had only gone for a few years to receive my education at university then I returned and was hired as estate manager to Lord James Pearl. Now that man, I can tell you, had more enemies than the good lord has angels. He was a cruel and selfish man; bitter and angry at and with everyone. There was never a need for him to fire the employees here, they all quit except for Jessop and Elizabeth. God only knows why they stayed and put up with him."

"Yet you were his estate manager?" Holmes asked.

"Yes, but I was hired by Winston Pearl, Mr. Holmes. I very rarely had dealings with the old man and on those few occasions that I did, I can tell you if it was not for Winston Pearl, I would have packed my bags and left with the rest of them."

"And you, Dr. Farley? Anyone you can think of that might have a grudge or wish the Pearls dead?" Holmes asked, turning to the doctor.

"No I cannot. But I have only been doctor here for the last fifteen years. I had no dealings with Lord James Pearl until Winston and his wife Dorthea arrived. Then I was called in because she had been taken to bed due to her pregnancy. It was also about that same time that Lord Pearl suffered his first heart attack. Or so it was the first heart attack that I knew about. I attended him and found him a cruel and foul tongued individual as Mr. Upland stated, It is a wonder Lady Pearl was able to put up with him."

"I see."

"Of course, once the boy was born things changed. The old man took to him as though he were his own. He frequently visited in the nursery, shooing the nanny out

125

of the room on those visits. He would sit for hours holding the baby, talking to him as though he could understand his every word. I think that he bonded with the child like he never did with his own. The boy, of course, loved his grandfather because to him he was always kind and loving. That's why Lord Pearl left the estate to the lad."

"So it is common knowledge that James Pearl left his own son with nothing."

"Yes, everyone knew. Everyone felt for Winston Pearl, but their pity was more because the old man was his father rather than that the old man left him out of the will."

"I wonder why," Watson remarked.

"Why what, Dr. Watson?" Farley asked.

"It does seem strange that the old man would leave his own son with nothing yet sign over his entire estate to a child, a grandson. What sort of rift was between James Pearl and his son that would cause that."

"I think you may be on to something there, Watson," Holmes said.

"Well," Farley said rising. "I only came to be sure Lady Pearl was well. Knowing that, I will take my leave and allow you to enjoy the remainder of your breakfast."

"Just one more thing, Dr. Farley," Holmes said. "Was there a nanny for the boy."

"Yes, a dear sweet old woman who came in on my recommendation to take care of Lady Pearl during her lay-in. She stayed to help with the boy until he was nearly four years old. Apparently there was a situation with the old man and she left abruptly, and has never been heard of or seen again."

"Do you by chance remember her name?"

"Yes. it was Ruth Charbane a sweet old woman. Nobody ever knew what happened to her. She just up and left one day. Well if that is all, I must be on my way. Good day." Farley picked up his hat and coat and left.

"And you, Mr. Upland?" Watson asked.

"I was thinking that if you would care to investigate some of the coves and bays today, Dr. Watson, I have the time. My business with Lady Pearl can hold until she has recuperated somewhat."

"I don't think today is…."

"Why not, Watson? You have maintained a solitary vigilance these many days and are deserving of a rest. I will be here and if help is needed, Angus is near at hand. Go enjoy yourself. It will do you good. Fresh air and all that."

"Well then, Mr. Upland, it is settled. Shall we have breakfast? I will change my clothes and put on some more appropriate footwear."

"Very good. I will have Justine pack us a light lunch then we will be ready."

"Very good."

Several minutes later, Watson and Upland were hiking across the pasture towards the cliffs. "We have to cross here then take a southerly direction. Just before the forest is a path that winds its way down the cliffs. It is fairly dangerous if one is not accustomed to such things. But we will go slow and watch your step," Upland said.

"That must be the path Lady Pearl and I could see from the ridge over there." Watson pointed to where he and Dorthea Pearl had strolled earlier.

"Yes it is. Lovely view, up there."

"It most certainly is," Watson said. "You stated you've lived here all your life. Born here, as a matter of fact."

"Yes. In my twenty-nine years of living in Cadwith, not much has changed. The people still fish for a living. Gray Manor still owns all the lands for a hundred miles or more. The small farms and cottages you see all belong to Gray Manor. They are rented out and the manor still collects not only rents but a portion of the crops."

"Twenty-nine? So you were not yet born when Winston Pearl was?"

"No that was several years before me. All I ever heard was that his mother died during childbirth and the old man was left with the child to raise."

"I see. Lady Pearl mentioned that her husband reduced the rents recently?"

"Yes. Lord Pearl was a kind and generous man. Once his father died, Winston became the Lord despite what the will said. He began fixing the place and was generous not only with his money but with his time to the people in the village. It was a sad day when his body was found on the beach. A sad day indeed."

"Indeed."

"Here we are at the path. Mind your step now, Dr. Watson."

"Mr. Upland!" Watson called out. "What is that just there?" he pointed to a dark opening below.

"Cave!" Upland called over his shoulder. "This particular beach has a very deep channel with a sandbar running along the cliffs just there. Pirates frequented this inlet years ago. They could sail their ships in just far enough to be protected by the cliffs. There's plenty of room to anchor and the water is clear enough to know your passage."

"So you think they used that cave there?"

"Absolutely. That cave has been investigated by nearly every boy and girl who grew up in Cadwith. There have been a few trinkets found, some pieces of gold, but nothing that would make anyone rich."

"I'd like to take a look inside, if that is all right with you?"

"Of course. Just another ten feet or so is a path that will take us there. As I said, everyone has had a hand in searching that cave. We won't find much else there but rocks and sand."

"Rocks and sand are fine with me." Watson followed Upland who now turned to his left. The path had leveled and was wide enough for two people to walk abreast of each other. Watson caught up with Upland. "How much further to the beach?"

"Not far. Forty more feet but the path veers to the left you can see just there," Upland pointed, "and will take us on a much safer path to the beach below."

"Oh my!" Watson stopped and looked at the gaping hole in the side of the cliff. "It is much larger than I thought."

"Yes, it is quite large inside. There are tunnels that go off in several different directions. I've explored several of them and they go on for miles it seems. I think the pirates really wanted to keep their treasure safe."

"They must have been successful if none has been found," Watson said. He stepped into the cave and was immediately struck by a strong cold wind that rushed forth from the interior of the cave. The angle of the opening prevented the sun from penetrating too far inside and he waited for his eyes to adjust. He walked about where the ground had been cleared of all rocks and other debris. Twenty paces inside, he could just make out a tunnel leading off his right and one in front. He circled the entire cave and found two more tunnels from his left.

"I think the next time we come we shall bring some torches. I would very much like to investigate these tunnels. Ah, what is this?" he bent to pick up a shiny object from the ground.

"Found some gold did you?" Upland asked.

"No indeed. Merely a button."

"Probably one of the children lost it. Can't say when. They come here all the time. Are you ready to go the rest of the way down?"

"Indeed. I have found my treasure. After you," Watson smiled and tucked the button absentmindedly into his pocket.

Several minutes later they stood on the beach looking out into the channel. "It is lovely here," remarked Watson.

"Yes. This was Lord and Lady Pearl's favorite spot. They would bring Daniel here to fish and swim. Up ahead just past that jutting rock is another small cove. That is where they found Lord Pearl's body."

"You don't say? Can we go there?"

"Yes of course. It is but a short distance."

"I was led to believe by Lady Pearl that his body was found quite some distance from here. Washed by the tide waters, she said."

"No, Lord Pearl and Daniel had come to fish that Sunday. Lady Pearl was ill and did not go. Their small boat was usually kept here in this bay but was found just a few feet from the cove where his body was discovered. Around the sand bar there," Upland pointed.

"Here we are. Doesn't look much now. The tides have washed away any traces of prints from the body and search party. But he was found here, his leg was wedged in this coupling of rocks. Probably washed in with the tide and caught his leg. At least that's what the inquest determined. That's why he didn't get washed back out with the outgoing tide."

"Here you say. In these rocks?"

"Yes, just there."

"I don't understand. If they set out fishing a mere hundred yards away, why did it take three days to find him here?" Watson asked.

"Tides around here do strange things. We think the tide swept him out and then washed him back in. That appears to be the only explanation," Upland shrugged. "The one accepted at the inquest."

"And he was so disfigured as to be unrecognizable?"

"So I was told. I did not find him. Rollie Fitzgibbons, a farmer here and a member of the search party found him. The man was badly shaken, I can tell you. Said he couldn't recognize the face at all, it had been battered by the rocks you see."

"Then how did they determine it was Winston Pearl?"

"His clothes, the ring on his finger. Winston Pearl always wore the ring of the Gray crest. It belonged to his mother you see."

"Yes, I'd forgotten that she was a Gray."

"It was a sad and tragic day when Winston Pearl died."

"Yes it was."

"Come on then. We have much more beach to explore. More caves and many more cliffs."

"What of this man, Rollie Fitzgibbons? Is it possible for Holmes and I to speak with him?"

"I'm afraid not. He was so terribly shaken he drank himself in a stupor one evening and lost his footing while walking back from Cadwith to his farm. He was found in the rocks just there." Upland indicated an area several feet further down the slope.

"Looks to be a dangerous trail," Watson murmured.

"Yes, it can be. Are you ready?"

"Lead the way my good man, lead the way."

Watson arrived at the dining table several minutes late, walking in with all eyes upon him. "It's good of you to join us, old chap," Holmes said.

"Sorry. Have I held up dinner? I do apologize."

"Nonsense," Dorthea said. "It has only been a few minutes. Conrad, you may serve now."

"Yes, Lady Pearl."

"And I see you are feeling much better, Dorthea?" Watson queried.

"I am indeed much better, thank you. So did you enjoy your explorations today, John?" she asked.

"Indeed I did. Mr. Upland has so much information about Cadwith."

"And did you find your treasure?" Dorthea smiled at him.

"Why yes, as a matter of fact I did. We had gone into a cave and I found this button just lying there." Watson reached into his pocket and pulled out the small ivory button. He held it in his outstretched hand.

The blood drained from Dorthea Pearl's face. "Oh no! It can't be! It just can't be!" She put out a shaking hand and picked up the button. "Oh, John, this is Daniel's button. Oh, it is my Daniel's button!"

"Where exactly did you find it, Watson?" Holmes rose to look at the button.

"It was just inside the cave, perhaps ten or fifteen feet."

"It looks clean and see here," Holmes turned the button over in Dorthea's hand. "The threads remain on the button, although shredded and loose, as if they had been torn away."

"Oh no!" Dorthea cried.

"Holmes!" Watson cried. "Must you?"

Holmes lowered his eyes, looking properly chastised. "I do apologize, Lady Pearl. It's the investigator in me."

Dorthea looked pleadingly at Watson. "May I have it, John?"

"Of course, my dear." Dorthea clasped it in her hand and held it tightly.

"Look," Watson said changing the subject. "As I said, Mr. Upland has told me much of Cadwith. He told me that the entire town was established more than two centuries ago on the whims of one man. A man by the name of Hebercomb Gray. I wonder, was he a relation?"

"I really don't know, John. Winston did not speak too much of his past. There are the paintings of the previous owners of Gray Manor along the walls in the foyer but there was never too much mention of them. But I believe there is a book somewhere in the library that has written a genealogy of the ancestors of Gray Manor. Perhaps one of these evenings we should look for it."

"Perhaps we should," Holmes said. "Perhaps this evening."

Dorthea give Holmes a most quizzical look, "If you wish. But first we shall finish dinner. Justine would be upset if we did not."

"I agree. After the day I've had in the fresh air, I am simply famished," Watson said. "By the way, Holmes. Has that mariner case been taken care of?"

"Yes, completed, with exactly the results we had anticipated."

"That is good. Any further cases at hand?"

"No, just this one."

"Now I am considered a case?" Dorthea asked. "On the train John called me a patient, now I am a case. This would be fairly amusing if the circumstances were not so.....sad."

"Regardless what we call you, Lady Pearl, the outcome will be the same. We will solve this situation and you will see that there is a logical explanation for everything that has happened. As I have always stated to Watson, there is a logical explanation for everything. One must simply look at the facts."

"And what facts have you determined thus far?" Dorthea asked.

Holmes pushed his plate forward. "There is the fact that someone wants you dead."

"Holmes!" shouted Watson.

"Oh, John, he is right. These are things I must face. What else."

"There is the fact that whoever it is has a very good command of the Gray estate layout not to mention an excellent command of a means of escape. Two very important things that Watson and I are looking into. The reason for this person's quest is as yet, unknown."

"You say person although it was definitely a man who tried to choke me in the fountain the other night."

"Yes, but I do not think he is working alone. I believe he has an accomplice; someone here who keeps him abreast of your day to day activities. Else how would he know you had gone to London? More important, how would he know where to look for you once you had arrived there?"

"You mean to tell me that I had been followed all the way to London? That the faces I'd been seeing and voices I'd been hearing were not my imagination but that of the man who followed me there?"

"Exactly what I am saying. What you are seeing and hearing is not an apparition, Lady Pearl. It is a real and genuine person and that person wants you dead."

"Although we do have a fairly good guess, don't we Holmes?" Watson asked.

"We never guess at anything, Watson. Everything is based on facts and one fact that is evident is that conerning this estate."

"Gray Manor? You mean someone wants to kill me because of Gray Manor?" Dorthea cried.

"Not because of Gray Manor, Lady Pearl, *for* Gray Manor. As yet I have no sufficient proof or evidence to hold up in a court of law. Now, if we are all done eating, I suggest we retire to the library and search for that book."

"I agree. Let's search for the book. There may be something there that will shed some light on this matter." Watson held Dorthea's chair, an annoyed shake of his head at Holmes. Holmes shrugged.

"Put a few more lamps on, would you Watson? Do you have any idea what this book would look like, Lady

Pearl?" Holmes asked pouring them each a brandy in the library.

"No I do not know much about it at all for I have never seen such a book. Winston mentioned it once. He said he'd entered the library to look for sketches of the house and he saw his father quickly conceal a volume of great thickness and age. His father became very enraged at the intrusion so Winston withdrew from the library without even looking for the sketches."

"If the thing is really old, it might be bound in a soft leather. But I cannot say. In my perusal of the shelves for something to read I did not come across anything unusual," Watson said.

"Did you spend much time in the library?" Holmes asked Dorthea Pearl.

"No, I came for a book once or twice. Winston spent a lot of time here. He found the architectural sketches for the estate and spent hours going over them. He said there was much more hidden at Gray Manor than anyone knows."

"Did he say those exact words?" Holmes asked.

"Yes, is that significant?"

"Possibly."

"I wonder what he meant by that," Watson said.

"Then let's have a look. Didn't you tell me you found the sketches spread out on the desk, Watson?"

"Yes, they were just here......" Watson shifted books and papers around the desk and looked up, surprised. "They are gone!"

"Gone? That cannot be. No one ever comes in here, John."

"Are you sure they were on the desk, Watson?" Holmes once more shifted the books.

"Absolutely sure. I turned several pages over. There was the east wing on the top, and beneath that were sketches for the mausoleum and the landscaping outlay for the front of the house." Watson searched the drawers of the desk and even got down on his knees to check underneath. "They are simply not here. Vanished."

"They must be here somewhere. Perhaps Anne has been in here cleaning."

"Possibly, and we shall ask her in the morning."

"I wonder if you would mind, Mr. Holmes, John. I would like to retire early. This room is simply too depressing for me."

"Not at all, Lady Pearl. Watson and I will continue our search for the book," Holmes said.

"Oh, of course, but we do not know if it actually exists and you may be wasting your time."

"Then again, maube not," Holmes said.

"Yes, well, goodnight, Mr. Holmes, goodnight, John."

Dorthea left the two of them to their search. She mounted the stairs to her room, dismissing Merryn who was waiting at the door with Angus. Only when the door was closed did she open the palm of her hand and stare at the small white pearl button that had grown warm and comforting there. It *was* the small white pearl button that was on Daniel's shirt the morning that he and Winston had gone fishing. The small white pearl button that now gave her renewed hope that Daniel was still alive. She lay on the bed, her pictures of Winston and Daniel with her and carefully and lovingly placed the small white pearl button with them.

"We will search systematically, Watson. You begin to the left of the door and I will start to the right. Shift the books and be sure to check the back of the shelves. I have found that to be a very convenient hiding place for secrets. Oh, by the way. I have taken the liberty to post Angus at her door once more. Tomorrow I mean to have a search of her bedroom for I believe there is something odd with that room and I mean to find out."

"I will help you investigate that room also. I agree with you. There is something amiss there. I think it has something to do with the noises I have been hearing and the voices Dorthea is hearing. That man is getting into the house somehow."

"I agree, but for tonight let's concentrate on the library first. If we find that book it just may give us an indication of why someone would wish to destroy the Gray ancestors."

Holmes and Watson circled the room pulling books from their shelves, reaching and poking along the walls behind. Several hours later they had completed the downstairs, finding nothing. They went up to the loft and resumed their search but nearing four in the morning they were no more near to their goal than when they had begun.

Holmes sat down in the chair behind the desk. Watson did the same opposite him. "Hours upon hours and we have come up empty handed," Watson groaned.

"Not so. At least we know there are no secret compartments behind the books."

"Yes but aren't there always secret passages in these old houses? Particularly in the library? Why should Gray Manor be any different?" Watson said.

"By God you are right, Watson!" Holmes exclaimed. "We have been searching for a small compartment for the book, a safe of some sort when what we should have been looking for is a catch, a trigger mechanism that would open an entire wall or move a bookcase." Holmes jumped up with renewed energy and began his search once more. "See here, Watson, this wall leads to the hall so there would be nothing there. That wall borders the outside so there would be nothi……… hold on!"

"What is it Holmes?"

"Didn't you tell me that you heard noises, when you were in the library the other night?"

"Yes I did but…"

"Where were you standing, Watson! Quick, think. Where were you standing?"

Watson rose reluctantly from the comfortable chair and went to stand where he'd been that night. "About here, more or less. I remember because I could see this shelf of books by the light coming through the window there. The noise was above me somewhere it seemed." Holmes quickly mounted the stairs to the loft.

"Yes, yes look here, Watson. This is a perfect ruse for a reading nook. Look where the bench ends. There is a three foot section of wall that contains….nothing. There has got to be something… a catch release…." but their search still netted them nothing.

"See here Holmes. You may continue searching as I know you will but I am going to retire. I will fetch you in the morning. Goodnight, Holmes."

"Ummm, yes, goodnight, Watson."

Watson trudged up the stairs and was about to enter his room when he decided to look in on Dorthea. Angus sat in his chair and nodded as Watson quietly opened the door. The bed was empty!

Watson threw the door open and ran inside, careful to check every corner of the room. Dorthea Pearl was not there. He was in the hall ready to shout for Holmes when Angus indicated, with a nod of his head, down the hall. He heard weeping then and followed until he found its source. Pushing open the door, he saw that he was in Daniel's room.

Dorthea was sitting in a rocking chair staring out a window. In her hand she held a small shirt pressed to her face. On the table nearby was the small pearl button. Watson closed the door quietly behind him and stood in the hall for a very long time. Oh, how he remembered doing the same thing. Missing Mary so deeply, so intensely, that the only way to sooth himself was to be near her things. To hold her nightdress to his face, to smell her still there with him. To touch her pillow, the side of the bed where she slept, gently caress the few strands of hair left on her brush. Close his eyes and pretend she was still there. Watson remembered the agony of her loss, the devastation of his happiness and tears rose to his eyes. He wiped them away with the back of his hand and left Dorthea Pearl to her memories.

Chapter Ten

The following day was raining and cold. Blue tentacles of lightening streaked across the dark clouds that crowded the sky followed by thunderous claps that shook the earth. Dorthea spent most of the day in her room, in her bed, beneath her blankets. She did not wish to see anyone. Not even John Watson. She thought of the voices that haunted her night dreams, of the apparitions that hung in the shadows, apparitions that only appeared when she was alone. She thought of the man in the fountain that looked so much like Winston in every respect but for the anger that emanated from his very soul and he had tried to kill her. A voice, a mere whisper, crept through the fog of her pain and hissed in her ear, was it Winston? Was he really trying to kill her? Her consolation was the small white pearl button she held clasped in her hand.

By early evening the rain finally ceased but the wind kept up its howling and Dorthea could stand the walls closing in upon her no more. She appeared in the door of the library with her shawl.

"Would anyone like to accompany me on a walk before dinner?"

"This late?" Watson asked checking his pocket watch.

"I know it is late and we will be dining soon, but I have to rouse myself out of this lethargy and the rain has stopped and I so desperately feel that I need some fresh air. Still searching for the book, Mr. Holmes?"

"Yes I am, so I hope you will forgive me not accompanying you."

"Not at all."

"Give me a moment and I will fetch my overcoat." Watson turned from the room. He returned and he and Dorthea set off arm in arm for a stroll about the grounds.

After a moment Dorthea said, "I know you have been worried about me, today, John. You must not think anything of it. There are days when I am most sad and feel so utterly alone and do not wish any company at all. My staff understand this and respect my wishes."

"Yes I was concerned. And my concern is growing, Dorthea; not only for your physical health but also for your mental health. You must try to work yourself back into a life. Become interested in your gardening, your needlework, something. It really does not do any good to think constantly over your loss."

"I know, and I do try. It's difficult because Winston and Daniel are my whole life and without them I feel I cannot be interested in anything ever again. My way is lost, John. I walk about constantly and am reminded of them everywhere I turn. They are there playing in the maze. They are there laughing throwing water at each other in the fountain. They are there racing ahead of me along the beach. It is so difficult to put those pictures out of my mind when I so long to never forget them."

"I understand. I truly understand. With time…"

"Yes with time."

"Ah, I see you are still enjoying your stroll. I thought I might join you after all. What say we take a turn through the maze?" Holmes approached them.

"Grand idea. Do you feel up to it, Dorthea?"

"I would love to."

The three of them walked casually through the maze. Here and there, Holmes stopped, taking an acute interest in the growth of a particular area. Overhead, the black clouds returned once more. "Come let us return. It feels as though the wind has gotten colder," Holmes remarked.

"Yes it has. And you are shivering, my dear." Watson removed his overcoat and placed it about her.

The long curtains on the windows had been closed early against the chill wind that whistled down from the moors. They retired to the drawing room and Dorthea sat near the fire, the chill of the brisk walk still enveloping her. Holmes was pouring drinks and Watson had already sat to light his pipe. "Conway? Please have Gwinn fetch more wood for the fire. I simply cannot rid myself of this chill."

"Perhaps you should not have accompanied Watson for that walk, Lady Pearl," Holmes remarked handing her a glass of sherry.

"But I enjoyed it. John has told me of your interest in solving puzzles, riddles, crimes and mysteries. I do hope you enjoyed it."

"Very much so. I find solving perplexing problems produces a keener mind; more alert, more aware."

"In what way, Mr. Holmes."

"I have always believed that the more one observes what is around him, the more natural it is to decipher and detect facts. Take for instance the maze. Watson told me that upon his arrival he stood for quite some time looking over the maze from his room. Now that being the perfect vantage point, he should have been able to determine the proper course to exit rather quickly. But he did not. He admitted that it had taken him quite some time. The reason for this is that he was following one path, one turn at a time when he should have been fixing his attention on the whole of the maze. At a glance he would have been able to circumvent the false paths redirecting his attention to the correct route."

"I do not know that you would have done much better, Holmes. After all it is a rather complex affair," Watson defended himself.

"On the contrary, Watson. I would have quickly cast an eye over the entire complex, subconsciously noting the false paths and straight away determined the course to follow. It is always better to have a complete knowledge of something and determine a course of action than to stumble through one phase at a time."

"But don't you feel there are times when one step at a time is the best course to follow?"

"Yes, in some cases, but in point of fact, not this one."

"Oh dear, I do hope I have not created a rift between you two?" Dorthea cried.

"Not at all. Holmes and I frequently banter back and forth. It is his way of stimulating conversation as well as thought," Watson said.

"So, Mr. Holmes, do you believe it is in the best interests of this case to take it step at a time or do you already have the entire case thought out in your head?" Dorthea asked.

"This particular case, I must admit has some intriguing aspects of which I have not made a final determination as of yet."

"I know you find me a fool to see and hear the things I hear and see. Oh thank you, Gwinn, put them directly on the fire and fetch me a shawl would you please?"

"I do not find you a fool, Lady Pearl for I believe you truly believe you are seeing and hearing these ghosts and voices. And may I remind you that the incident in the water fountain has proven they are not ghosts but real human beings. Human beings that wish you harm."

"Perhaps you should have a séance, Lady Pearl. That gypsy woman that passes through Cadwith with the rest of the caravan travelers has set her tent at the edge of town. Me and Angeline went to see her the other day and she told us our fortunes, she did. She said that Angeline would soon be wed and have lots of children and wouldn't you know the next day that boyfriend of hers asked her to marry him!"

"Stop that utter nonsense, Gwinn," Watson said. "Lady Pearl does not wish to hear it nor have it mentioned again."

Gwinn looked startled and she curtseyed to the floor. "I beg pardon, my Lady, I meant no disrespect, but she is good! She told us what was going to happen and it did! I meant no disrespect, my Lady," she cried.

"Let us not mention it again shall we?" Watson said.

"Wait, I…I do wish to hear of this gypsy woman."

"Dorthea you cannot be serious?"

"I am, John. I have had these dreams, these nightmares, the visions and hearing the voices ever since the accident. Even allowing for that night in the fountain that there is actually someone out there wanting to hurt me, I…I simply cannot go on not knowing whether Daniel is alive or dead. In my head I think he is dead but that is only because everyone is telling me it must be so. But in my heart I know he is still alive for every ounce of my being as a mother tells me that it is so. He is calling out to me, he tells me he is frightened and I must find him, I must know the truth, John, else I will not be able to go on!" Dorthea cried.

"This might solve some issues, Watson. Perhaps we should make arrangements to visit this gypsy woman," Holmes said.

"You must be joking! Holmes! You?" Watson cried.

"Logically, Watson, if Lady Pearl is able to derive some satisfaction from her visit than I think it should be done."

"Oh thank you, Mr. Holmes. I am not a believer in such things but I am at my wits end and am willing to try anything to learn the truth. I know deep down you believe this to be the ravings of a mad woman. I have listened to the police and they have told me Daniel is dead despite not having found his body. I have listened to you and John and although I know you are still investigating the matter, still have not determined anything specific or real to explain what is happening. I need answers, you see. I need answers now."

"I understand, Lady Pearl. Let's have Gwinn make the arrangements for this gypsy woman to come to the house, say tomorrow night?" Holmes said.

Gwinn exclaimed. "I would be happy to Mr. Holmes. I can go to the village in the morning."

"Yes please do. Whatever she requests, let it be done."

"Yes sir, I surely will." Gwinn curtsied once more and left quickly, excited over the prospect of seeing the gypsy once more.

"Gwinn! Send Merryn in, I am ready to retire for the evening. I hope you gentlemen will excuse me, goodnight."

"Good night, Lady Pearl," Holmes bowed to her.

"Good night Dorthea. If there is anything you need?" Watson said escorting her to the door where Merryn was waiting.

"No thank you, Merryn is all I need right now. Good night."

Watson watched as the two women crossed the hall and mounted the stairs. When they were out of hearing, he turned angrily on Holmes. "What the hell do you think you are doing? That woman is in a fragile state as it is and you pull a stunt like this?"

"I am not doing anything nor am I pulling any sort of stunt, Watson. It is what the lady wishes. You yourself should understand how grief works. First there is the hurt, a painful and agonizing pain that surrounds your entire being. One cannot think, eat, sleep or gain any respite from the emptiness that once was a happy life.

"Then comes the anger and hatred where one blames the departed for leaving them, blames those about them for not doing more, and finally blames himself for something, anything, they might have done or said that would have, could have, should have, prevented the loss. People do not mourn for the lost one, Watson, they mourn for themselves because they are alive and must live with a guilt that is made up in the mind because the mind cannot fathom that loss without self-blame. She needs someone, even if it is a gypsy, to tell her she is not to blame."

"But you and I have both told her this, Holmes."

"Yes and we are her friends. She expects us to say such things. But a stranger, that is a different influence altogether. Lady Pearl needs the reassurance of this woman to ease her mind, settle her conscience and in that respect I think the voices and ghosts will stop."

"But I thought you said she was in real danger?"

"She is, but not from ghosts."

"But, then, what is all this about, Holmes? First you say she is in real danger, then you say she is seeing ghosts and hearing voices? One cannot be if the other exists."

"Yes, it most certainly can. There is a real danger here because there is someone in Lady Pearl's past or her husband's that is manipulating her state of mind using the death of her husband and son to rid Gray Manor of her. They are using the guise of ghosts and whispers in the dark to achieve their purpose."

"For what reason?"

"I do not know yet, but I have learned that the midwife who attended to Lady Anna Pearl, Winston's mother, is still alive. She has moved and now resides up north in a place called Steverton. I have made plans to go. But first we will attend the séance and quite possibly we will learn something."

The following evening, Madam Saphera, as the gypsy woman called herself, arrived promptly at eight. Watson and Holmes were speaking quietly with Arthur Upland and Dr. Farley, both had been called upon to sit in at the séance.

Madam Saphera looked about the room then set about quickly laying out her materials before her. She chanted in hushed tones as she did so. A small circle of ash was drawn out on the table and two large candles placed precisely spaced inside with a large crystal of sparkling blue between them. On the outside of the ash circle, was the vial of special oil that she poured into a small silver bowl and another of salt that lay in a silver urn. She looked up when Dorthea entered.

"Lady Pearl, it is my pleasure to meet you and enter your lovely home. I sense there is much sadness here, much loss. There are two items I will need from you. I must have a few strands of hair and a recent item that was touched by your loved one."

"There are two," Dorthea swallowed and whispered to her.

"Two?" Madam Saphera inquired.

"Two, yes. Two loved ones."

"I see. Then I shall need these items for each of them, and I will be ready to begin."

"I will fetch them. Merryn, please see that the others are seated and I will return promptly."

Dorthea hurried away. Upstairs, some hair taken from Winston's brush on the dressing table and the Gray crested ring that had been found on the body. In the boys room, Daniel's favorite riding cap with strands of hair caught in the brim, and the pearl button, the button found by Watson she so cherished as her last hope. She hugged the items to her and returned where she handed them to Madam Saphera.

Dorthea took the seat next to her and Holmes took a seat directly opposite Madam Saphera with Watson to his right. Dr. Farley was directly on his left with Arthur Upland next to the doctor. Madam Saphera lay the ring near one of the candles, the button near the other. Taking the few strands of Winston's hair, she dipped first into the oil then the salt. She passed the hair through the candle flame and it hissed and sizzled into ash where she let it fall on the ring.

Daniel's hair she raised to her nose first, then dipped it into the oil, then the salt. Passing it through the second candle, she let the ash fall onto the small button that lay there. She then reached her hands out grasping Upland's and Dorthea's, the movement causing the flames of the candles to waver. "Please join hands. I must insist that whatever happens, no matter what transpires, it is through me and I have no control. I must ask that you all remain silent else I will not be able to hear the spirits that wish to communicate."

Watson looked at Holmes with a skeptical roll of his eyes and shook his head. He was set against the nonsense of a séance fearing not only Dorthea's physical health but her state of mind. How Holmes could sanction such a preposterous gathering was beyond his wildest imagination.

Holmes stared back at Watson, leaned to him and whispered, "We need answers, Watson."

"Answers? Answers to what?" Watson hissed back. "This is the most ludicrous idea you have come up with yet, Holmes!"

"Quiet please," Madam Saphera said. "I sense there are non-believers at our table, but that is of no consequence. There is belief in the one that matters. We must all close our eyes. Allow the spirit world to envelope our beings, enter this room and our minds. We must open our minds and let them enter." She closed her eyes and put her head down, her chin coming to rest upon the bloodstone, a large round pendant of polished jasper peppered with red flecks that hung about her neck on a large silver chain.

"Winston Pearl we are searching for you. For you and Daniel. Winston Pearl can you hear us. Can you see past the darkness of your resting place? Can you come into the light? Winston Pearl can you come to us? Speak to us? Dorthea is here, Winston. Dorthea is here and wishes to speak with you, wishes to know you are safe and happy, Winston. Can you come to us? Can you tell us what happened?"

Silence filled the room and they waited. Holmes opened his eyes and looked around at those at the table. They sat holding hands, their faces lined with anxious hope that an answer would come. But the room remained silent. He closed his eyes once more.

"Daniel," Saphera whispered. "Daniel can you speak with us? Are you here with us Daniel? Can you come into the light and speak with your mother? She is here Daniel. She is here waiting for you, longing for you, loving you Daniel. She holds your ivory button in her hand. The button you lost that day of fishing with your father. Can you come into the light and speak to us?"

Again the room filled with silence and they waited. "Daniel. Please spea.....wait...I see, I see a child. A child... a boy. He is there, in the darkness, in the darkness alone and afraid. He is a small child, crying into the night, Mama, Mama, please come Mama."

"Daniel!" Dorthea.cried out.

"Hush, Lady Pearl, we must not break the connection. Daniel is here, he wishes to...wait. It is still there. I can still see him. Daniel is there in the dark. He lies with a blanket on a small cot. The room is dark and cold, cold and damp. He...wait, he is clutching something.... something in his hand. Holding it tight to his chest. I...I can not see what it is. Daniel!" Saphera whispered, "You must move, you must allow us to see what it is you have in your hand. The boy moves, he is holding something, wait…I can see it now. Daniel, I see you are not alone. You have something, someone there with you? Daniel?" Saphera called, "Daniel! It is there, I can see it now, it is a hand. The hand of a…a man, a man lying on the floor…. It is….wait…'Mama, Mama,' Daniel cries once more and the hand rises to stroke the boy's face.

"Mama will find us, my son. We must hold on. We must not give up hope. The man speaks reassuring the boy. I can see him, I can see the man comforting the boy, holding him now…he cries into the night, 'Dorthea, Dorthea we are here? Why do you look for us among the dead? We are not. You must follow the path through the wall of shadows, beneath the tombs of darkened earth. We are here, Dorthea, waiting!'"

"Winston? Daniel?" screamed Dorthea. She threw Madam Saphera's hand from her and pulled away from Watson. Wild eyed and hysterical, she screamed into the darkness, flailing her arms about her. "Winston! Winston where are you, where is Daniel? You have given us a riddle and I cannot find you?"

Watson rushed to take hold of Dorthea but she pushed him aside and darted about the room, knocking things over, throwing objects to the floor, screaming for Daniel and Winston. Holmes and Upland rose from their chairs and between the three of them, managed to hold and subdue Dorthea.

"Look what you've done?" shouted Watson at Madam Saphera.

"I have done nothing the Lady did not wish for," Madam Saphera said. "You have been searching among the dead. Obviously this is not so."

"Watson, help me get her to her bed," Dr. Farley shouted. "She must be sedated immediately before she injures herself!"

"Step aside," ordered Upland who scooped her into his arms and with Farley leading the way he carried her to her room.

"I'll fetch my valise," Watson cried. "I have a sleeping potion that will work quickly."

Saphera blew out her candles, replaced the oil back into the vial, then returned it and the candle and the silver urns into her bag. She closed the lid and stood. "I must go. My work here is done. I will tell you that I have seen another, another who is as Winston. Find him and you will find the man and the boy. The rest is up to you, Sherlock Holmes. Winston and Daniel call out for help and help you must. Look no longer in the land of the dead but turn your energies to the living."

"But…" Holmes began.

"Stop!" Madam Saphera held her hand to silence him. "That is all I can say." She left him standing with unanswered questions on his lips.

It was more than an hour before Watson entered into the drawing room, his face still flushed and angry. Holmes sat near the now roaring fireplace, smoke billowing from his pipe. "I do hope Lady Pearl is resting?"

"Finally," Watson sighed. "I will have a brandy. A very large brandy. You?"

"Yes, thank you Watson. I apologize for any discomfort Lady Pearl has experienced."

"Discomfort? Discomfort you call it?" Watson handed Holmes a glass. "She was ranting out of her mind, Holmes! Thank goodness Farley was here. He is staying the night, keeping watch on her to be sure she sleeps through."

Watson paced the room sidestepping the shards of broken crystal and puddle of lamp oil saturating the floor. "How did she know all of that, Holmes? How did she know their names? How did she know our names? How did she come to see that they are not dead?" He finally sat opposite Holmes and said. "I've had time to think and I want you to know I really do not blame you, Holmes. You are correct. It is what Dorthea wished. I think she did not know exactly what was to happen and was not prepared for the results."

"We were not prepared either, Watson. The results may have set her into a state of hysteria but it did give us a new direction. According to the gypsy woman we have been searching in the wrong places. Instead of searching for the perpetrator of her ghosts and voices, we should set our goal on finding Daniel."

"Daniel?"

"Yes, for he is still alive."

"You believe so?"

"I do. No body was ever found; nothing save the button you found in the cave. Also, we should verify that the body buried in the Gray Mausoleum is truly that of Winston Pearl. I am sure Madam Saphera has heard the entire story of their deaths in the village, as you know how gossip spreads. That is a simple fact and not a mystical vision by a gypsy woman."

"Very likely true, Holmes. But you are not suggesting that the body is not that of Winston Pearl?"

Watson cried. "But surely Dr. Farley would not play foul with Dorthea?"

"Not intentionally, Watson. But Lady Pearl herself told us that his body had been in the water for several days and was so badly disfigured by the rocks and water that he was unrecognizable. It may be that even the good Dr. Farley was unsure or was unable to identify the body. Hence the reason why he had Lady Pearl verify the clothes and the ring."

"That would mean someone went to a lot of trouble to have everyone believe the body found was that of Winston Pearl."

"There may be more to the madness than we realize. I have been contemplating the riddle of the gypsy woman. Search through the wall of shadows, beneath the tombs of darkened earth. What does that suggest to you, Watson?"

"Wall of shadows, darkened earth, could mean anything. What could possibly be the wall of shadows? Beneath the darkened earth would mean underground. Buried. Buried beneath the ground."

"The wall of shadows? Beneath the darkened earth?" Holmes said aloud more to himself than to Watson. "The mausoleum? That's it, Watson, the mausoleum. The walls are constructed of stone and any light inside would cast shadows. The crypt is most likely buried underground some ten to twenty feet which would account for the 'beneath the darkened earth'."

"By golly, Holmes, you may be correct," Watson exclaimed.

"Quick, fetch some lamps," Holmes shouted and rushed from the room.

"What? Now? You wish to go now?" Watson shouted after Holmes retreating figure, knowing that was a hopeless gesture. He hurried to catch up.

Holmes led the way, his stride long and hurried with excitement. "We really do not need the light to find our way here," he said moving swiftly through the network of passages of the maze

"No there is a bright enough moon up there to show us the way."

"Yes, thank the stars for that, eh Watson?" Holmes laughed.

"Hold on?" Watson gripped him by the elbow. "You mean to tell me that was you in the coach? Holmes you scoundrel!"

"Of course, Watson. You do not think I would miss an opportunity to hone my skills at disguise do you? And yes, that first evening you were here, I saw you at your balcony while I was ascertaining the route through this maze. I know you saw me, but hoped you would attribute it to animals or simply an over active imagination."

"You? Again? Holmes you really must clue me in on what your plans are."

"You did not need to know at the time, and it was necessary I roam about inconspicuously. Ah, here we are, the end of the maze. There ahead is the path to the mausoleum. It is fairly well taken care of, thank Winston Pearl for that. I feel the mausoleum will give us the next clue to the puzzle."

The path curved and twisted rising slightly as they neared the funerary encampment of the Gray ancestors. After several minutes, they stepped on an open expanse of lawn bathed in moonlight. The foreboding presence of the mausoleum loomed before them like a giant gray ghost in the dark.

Unlike its Gray Manor counterpart, the mausoleum was cut from a solid block of pink quartz more than twenty feet high. To either side of the entrance stood large pedestals each topped with a stone statue. At its center was a set of doors and twisted around the handles was a chain and a lock.

"Damn it all!" cursed Holmes. "I didn't think it would be locked."

"I imagine it must be. Grave robbers abound whether it be here or in London, I am sure."

"Here," Holmes shoved his lantern into Watson's hand. He backtracked down the path for several feet until he found what he was looking for. Watson watched and wondered what Holmes was about until he saw him returning with a large stone in his hand.

"I see. Now we are to be the criminals? Breaking into the Gray tombs, come now, Holmes. This could wait until morning when we are able to obtain the key from Upland."

"Can't wait, Watson. We must find answers now, tonight. Each day that passes puts Winston and Daniel at more risk and I daresay after all these weeks and months of being held prisoner somewhere, they must be nearing their end."

"So you believe Madam Saphera?"

"I believe they are still alive. It is that which is the most logical explanation. I do not know who or why but someone has kidnapped Winston and Daniel and are holding them as captives. It is why Winston's body was unrecognizable and Daniel's was never found. It explains why Lady Pearl is not only hearing their voices but also seeing them. They are not spirits. They are real. They are being held captive and forced to do the kidnappers will because he is pitting the life of one against the other if they don't comply."

"But for what end, Holmes?"

"It's all about the money. It always is. The entire tragedy began when Winston took control of Gray Manor. Whoever it is, is trying to frighten Lady Pearl into believing they are ghosts. They are trying to convince her to join them, to kill herself, to be with them."

"But if they have kidnapped Winston and Daniel, why would they keep them alive all this while? Why not simply kill them at the start?"

"They are using them as a ransom of sorts, Watson. They are finding their way into the house somehow, sometimes using Winston, sometimes using Daniel. That would account for those times that Lady Pearl hears their voices because it is actually them calling out to her. That would account for why Lady Pearl sees them in the dark because they are really there. The kidnapper is employing a secret means of entrance and exit into the manor itself. What better place to hide that than in a mausoleum?"

"Ah, I finally understand. What a cruel and hideous trick to play upon someone. To slowly drive her insane, an insanity witnessed by all those about her until she can stand it no longer and takes her own life. No one would think twice of her death, would they?"

"No, and that is their objective. Once Lady Pearl is out of the way, they could simply and most likely would, do away with both Winston and Daniel as they would no longer be needed and are already pronounced dead."

"But if it is being done for the money, how are these kidnappers expected to get their hands on the estate?

After all Winston and Daniel were the last heirs to the inheritance."

"No, Winston and Daniel are, by all accounts already dead. Dorthea Pearl is the last remaining obstacle to gaining the inheritance. Once she has been dealt with, whoever it is can stake their claim."

"But who? Who could possible....."

"When you and Dr. Farley escorted Lady Pearl to her quarters, Madam Saphera said one more thing to me. She said there is one other as Winston. What do you suppose that means?"

Watson stared at Holmes. "That there is another heir?"

"Exactly, and one who is willing to kill to claim the inheritance! If this other heir makes all these deaths look like an accident, he can inherit freely. The courts will not question his coming forward to do so."

"I rather like your theory, Holmes. I was beginning to have doubts about Winston, truthfully."

"As was I. The thought had occurred to me that it actually was Winston trying to be rid of Dorthea, after all she said the man at the fountain looked and spoke like Winston. But for the life of me I could not fathom a reason why as he already had control of the estate."

"It may be he suffered the same mental state as his father. There are cases where the disease of the father is inherited by the children."

"And that is proven?" Holmes queried.

"Not exactly, not yet, but I have had cases where there are physical ailments that were suffered by the parent and have been passed to the children. What would make a physical ailment any different than a mental one?"

"You tell me, you're the doctor. Yet, I don't see that as the problem. Now that we've established another heir, therein lies our problem."

"Well, if what you say is correct, Holmes, then we had better get inside this tomb and find answers. Find answers before the kidnapper succeeds in driving Dorthea out of her mind."

Holmes smashed the stone on the lock until finally it snapped falling with a resounding clang to the stone below. He gripped the handle and pulled the heavy door open. Cool air rushed from the tomb, an air sick and sour with the smell of death, decay and age. Watson covered his face and handed Holmes the second lantern. Together they entered into the blackened depths of the Gray Mausoleum.

A landing of several feet, then more than twenty stairs took them down deeper into the depths of the earth. The inside of the tomb was quite large and coffins rested on pedestals around the entire thing. "Egan Matthew Gray, 1743," Watson read. "Elizabeth Mary Gray, 1744. Conan Lane Gray, 1755. These appear to be all children, Holmes."

"Over here, Watson. More recent we have Alden Middleford Gray, 1886. It says brother. Here is Farley Bartholomew Gray, 1888, brother. Ah, here is James Hawkins Garmen Pearl, Winston's father. Look around, Watson. I do not see ....ah here it is the tomb for Anna Eleanore Gray Pearl, Winston's mother."

"Do you suppose that this Alden Gray and Conan Gray could possible have had an heir who now wishes to inherit?"

"It is possible, and most likely. Search the walls, the crevices and recesses and don't forget those niches with the statues there. There must be some sort of catch, a latch to a hidden chamber that leads to the house."

"But already this makes no sense, Holmes. If the kidnapper is using the mausoleum as the means to enter the house, how is he getting in and out of it? As you very well know it was locked on the outside," Watson said.

"Damn! That is so. But that simply means there must be another tunnel leading to somewhere else or he has a set of keys. I am sure it starts here. Let's keep looking as long as we are already here. And don't forget the niches!"

Holmes and Watson scoured every inch of wall, every square foot of floor and found nothing. No footprints, no fingerprints, no dust. "Well, that puts an end to that theory, doesn't it?" Watson said coming back to rest near the tomb of Anna Eleanore Gray Pearl. He leaned back against the tomb and the lid shifted.

"What was that?" Holmes spun around at the sound.

"The lid. It moved!"

"But how can that be? That should be sealed. Here, give me a hand." Holmes gripped one edge and Watson the other. They pushed at the heavy slab and it slid further away from the top.

"Do you think we really should be doing this, Holmes? First you destroy the lock on the outside and now you are desecrating the tomb of Winston's mother!" Watson exclaimed.

Holmes lifted the torch and peered inside. "I don't think we are desecrating anything, Watson. She isn't here."

"What?" Watson peered into the coffin.

"She isn't here, but our carefully hidden book is."

"Is that the book of the Gray's? Here? What on earth?"

"It is the book, and my...my...my... the lost plans are here also. Hold up that lantern. Look here, the first entry. It reads June 27, 1645. Have arrived safely in the cove. Trunks of gold and jewels safely in cave. Must lie low. Weather the storm."

"Holmes, we can't read it here."

"Of course, we'll take it back to the library where we can do it proper justice."

"We may not have found a secret passage but we have found much more than that. So much for theories."

"Oh there may yet be a passage here despite the fact that there is no sign of a print or dust. Why?"

"You forget that Winston Pearl was buried here not more than four months ago. I am sure Dorthea had the place cleaned for the service."

"You are probably right. Let's get out of here." At the foot of the stairs, Holmes turned to look once more about the room. He shook his head and mounted the stairs behind Watson. "I am extremely angry with myself, Watson. I know this mausoleum is the first clue; the first link in the chain to finding Winston and Daniel. I am going to refresh my lantern and start anew."

"You don't mean now, Holmes? It is daybreak and we have been at it all night. You have not slept a wink. Furthermore, there is the book"

"I don't need sleep. What I need are answers and I will certainly sleep much better once I have them."

"As will we all. Come on then. Let's have a go at that book and then a couple hours rest . Then I will join you once again."

"Right."

Chapter Eleven

Back at the library, Holmes pulled the two chairs together and he and Watson sat with the book open before them. "All right, let's see what this book of secrets has to tell us, shall we Watson?" He began to read,

"'1645. We was all pirates on the ship *The Gray Lady*, Captain Hebercomb Hawkins being her captain. Tobias Roberts was his first mate and Jack Easton the second mate. Me? I was cook. Me name be Nathanial Ward. We was all on a run from Jamaica to Bristol when we ran into foul weather before reaching the ocean. Most supplies was washed overboard and the crew got real sick. We dumped bodies overboard every day, sometimes two, three men at a time. The captain calls us in. He got a plan. There weren't enough food for everyone and we was hauling twenty-two chests of gold and jewels that we was supposed to split amongst us. Captain Hawkins says that its three maybe four days to Bristol and he says we can make it with just four of us. We decided to kill everyone on board but us four that way we only had to split four ways. So we did. We run into bad weather and grounded in a small channel on the Cornish coast. No people for miles. No houses, nothing. Captain Hawkins says this was a good place to call home and we unloaded the chests into the row boats cause we found a cave to hide them in on shore. But when we was loading the last of the chests,

Tobias come up with this here idea to kill Hawkins then we'd only have to split three ways. So we did. We stabbed him and set a charge to blow the ship once we was back on shore.

"'July 18,1645. Been in the cave going on a month now. No sign of people so we been dividing the chests between me and Tobias and Jack. We don't want no one knowing who we are so we changed our names all to Gray. We was all from *The Gray Lady* anyhows. We says from now on we are brothers.

"'August 1, 1645. Tobias ain't come to the meal today. We been living off fish and birds. Not bad when the cookin is done right. Been three days and Tobias still ain't come back. We went to look. The cliffs are steep and dangerous. If he got himself killed, me and Jack are gonna split his share.

"'August 6, 1645. We found Tobias. He weren't killed by no fall. There was a stab hole going clean through his heart. Me and Jack are worried. But we split Tobias' chests between us anyhow.

"'August 17, 1645. Found Jack today. He had his throat cut clean from ear to ear. Now the gold and jewels is all mine but am too scared to leave the cave. The birds are hard to catch and haven't eaten in two days. Found a couple a rats and ate them. Terrible but at least I am safe in the cave.

"'September 1, 1645. Today Nathanial Ward died at my hand. The three pirates killed my crew, tried to kill me, destroyed my ship and stole our plunder. Vengeance was mine. Now the gold and jewels are all mine. I will build here, marry here and die here. My name is now Hebercomb Hawkins Gray.'"

Watson eased back into his chair and stared at Holmes. "So what Upland said was true. This Hebercomb Gray was the first settler to Cadwith."

"Yes, he appeared to be a fair sort, for a pirate. Justice was served and all that," remarked Holmes.

"Skip forward a bit. Looks like the next few pages are about the village and people coming to live here. There….." Watson stopped the page. "Right there."

"'July 21, 1680. Today my father Hebercomb Hawkins Gray has died. Yesterday he told me of this book and told me to keep the entries going. One day I must tell my son, Henry or Bartholomew whichever is to inherit Gray Manor. My brother Soames does not know of the book. He has no children. Perhaps one day."

"Skip ahead a few more pages, this appears to be family decendants," Watson said flipping the pages. "Ah, here looks like something interesting."

"'July 6, 1743, Egan Matthew Gray has died by strange means.' "Strange means? How can one not know how one dies?" Watson asked more to himself than to Holmes.

"'May 22, 1744 Elizabeth Mary Gray has died by strange means.'"

"Watson, something very peculiar is happening here. Take a closer look at these entries, dating as far back as the early 1700's. There are children that are dying strangely, mysteriously, and no one has any explanation for their death."

"Strange indeed, Holmes. Even a cursory look at a dead body should give some indication of death, whether it be by foul means or by disease."

"I agree. Let's read further."

Dorthea woke with a start. She lay in her bed, her heart pounding in her chest, her eyes darting about the room. The nightmare had been so real, as if Winston were standing there, holding her in his arms; holding her, kissing her, his hands at her throat, choking the breath out of her. She screamed and immediately Merryn rushed in. "Is everything all right, my Lady? I heard you cry out!"

"Oh Merryn, it was another nightmare. A strange nightmare that I have been afflicted with as of late."

"Are you wishing to rise, my Lady?"

"Yes, Merryn. Please ring for breakfast. I will dress and eat in my room."

"Yes my Lady, but that Mr. Sherlock Holmes has your best interests at heart. He says he and Dr. Watson wish to search in here." Merryn rang the bell to alert the kitchen then laid out clothes for Dorthea and went quickly to straighten the bed clothes.

"Have Mr. Holmes and John risen yet?" Dorthea asked.

"They are in the library, my Lady. They have not been to bed yet."

"What? Then I shall see to them first. Have a fresh pot of coffee put up and we will all be down in a few moments."

"Yes, my Lady."

"And what is so interesting that you have not slept, either of you?" Dorthea called upon entering the library.

Holmes closed the book and moved it out of view.

"We have been discussing our next strategy, that is all."

"You are a terrible liar, John. Surely you can do better than that. I did notice that book you pushed aside there. Is it perhaps the book of Gray secrets?"

Watson shrugged his shoulders and Holmes laughed. "You are quite the observer, Lady Pearl. As a matter of fact, yes it is."

"May I have a look at it?"

"No. I am going to ask you to trust me explicitly regarding the contents of this book. Watson and I need time to peruse through and determine just exactly what was going on throughout the rule of the Gray dynasty and I would particularly wish this book to remain a secret. We must not tell anyone we have found it, no mention to anyone else that it even exists."

"Sounds ominous, Mr. Holmes."

"I am afraid it is."

"If that is your wish, I shan't mention it again. At least until you do," Dorthea smiled. "Merryn has coffee and breakfast ready. Please. Won't you both join me?"

"Yes, but first allow me to put this book in a safe place. I will see you both downstairs shortly," Holmes said.

Watson put out his elbow to Dorthea who smiled and slipped her arm through. "After you," Watson said.

"Are you up to discussing the séance, Lady Pearl?" Holmes asked once they had retired outside. They sat near the fountain. Dorthea glanced at the fountain and shuddered.

"Yes, I must harden myself to these matters if we are to determine the truth, mustn't I, Mr. Holmes."

"Yes, I am afraid you must."

"Do you feel we might be more comfortable in the drawing room?" Watson asked.

"No, Watson, here is just fine," Holmes spoke quickly.

"I….I don't understand, Mr. Holmes," Dorthea said.

"There is something strange in that house, Lady Pearl. Someone somehow is always one step ahead of what we are up to. It may be one of your staff eavesdropping on our conversations, I don't know yet. However, we will take all precautions. I curse myself for not thinking of it with regard to the book."

"I can't believe it is one of my people," Dorthea sputtered, "but if you feel this is necessary, then by all means."

"Good. Now, did you or any one instruct Madam Saphera as to the past events in the house?"

"No, but I am sure it is on everyone's mind and tongue in the village. You yourself know how such things transpire."

"Yes, of course. And you, Watson. Had you told anyone of the button you found?"

"No, of course not. It was just a button after all. But Mr. Upland was there with me in the cave when I found it. He made little issue of the thing, Holmes."

"Do you have any thoughts as to what Madam Saphera meant by, the wall of shadows or tombs of darkened earth?"

"None what-so-ever. I must be honest, Mr. Holmes, that I was so caught up with what she said about Winston and Daniel still being alive that I failed to hear anything else that was being said. Do you think it is really true? Do you think they may still be alive? After all this time? And where would they be, why haven't they come back to me?" Dorthea cried.

"Dorthea, do not distress youself. We are trying to help. If you continue to let your emotions interfere with Holmes' investigations we will never move forward," Watson said soothingly, holding her hand.

"I am sorry," Dorthea replied. "It's the thought of them still alive, trapped somewhere, and I cannot find them."

"If they are still alive, Holmes will find them, you can count on that, Dorthea," Watson said. "But first we have to work through the riddle of Madam Saphera. We have to decipher what is in that secret book and we really must keep our wits about us."

"Well said, Watson."

"Do you think they really may still be alive, Mr. Holmes?"

"There is a possibility, but I do not wish to get your hopes up, Lady Pearl. Madam Saphera made several interesting observations that have shed new light on the case. It has opened up another avenue to pursue. What we need now is your full cooperation. You must do exactly as we say. Right now, I want you to stay here, at the manor. In the company of your maid, Merryn. Never be alone, Lady Pearl. I have instructed Angus to accompany you if you wish to be outdoors, but Merryn must be with you at all times indoors. Is that understood?"

"Yes, yes of course. But what of you and John?" she asked.

"Watson and I will look into one of these new lines of inquiry. I hope you can understand that nothing must be said regarding this at this time."

"I understand, Mr. Holmes. I will do as you say. Will you be requiring a carriage?"

"No, two saddled horses will be fine. It will appear we are simply going riding In this way there will be no means of forwarning those at our destination."

"Now it is you who speak in riddles, Mr. Holmes. But I will not say a word. I will have Angus saddle two of our best mounts."

"An easy rider for me, Dorthea. I am unaccustomed to riding, as you know," Watson said.

They left within the hour, riding in silence for several miles before Watson spoke.

"See here, Holmes. What was the necessity of the secrecy back there?"

"I took the opportunity in the library, when you and Lady Pearl went down together, to look over the sketches. It was as you suspected, Watson. There are a series of hidden walls within Gray Manor."

"Hidden walls?"

"Yes. They are only wide enough for the passage of one person at a time to pass through but enough to allow access to most of the rooms. There are even stair cases that connect the wings."

"Then someone has gained access to the manor through these hidden walls? That would account for the strange noises I was hearing yet not finding anything. Was there no indication on those plans to show where the outside entrance might be?"

"No there was not I am afraid. There was also no indication as to where in the house the intruder may be able to exit the hidden wall and gain access to the rooms of the house."

"So the key to how this intruder is entering the manor remains a mystery."

"Yes it does. Those walls also account for how Dorthea is able to hear and see her ghosts. They are not truly ghosts, Watson. There is a real body, somebody, that is moving about the house through those walls, seeing and knowing every move we make. He knows where the passages are in the house. Tomorrow we will definitely investigate Lady Pearl's room."

Watson pulled his mount up short. "Holmes!" he cried. "Do you think that is the meaning of Madam Saphera's wall of shadows?"

Holmes stared over the horses' rump. "By God, Watson, the walls. Of course! Damn! Why didn't that come to me?"

"Because we were concentrating on tunnels in the mausoleum, but…"

"Yes of course! The walls in the house; the tunnels in the mausoleum. That is our connection! That is how the killer is getting back and forth without being noticed. The walls in the house must connect to tunnels to the mausoleum. We simply have to find the entrance."

"That we might possibly never find. Perhaps it rests in the east wing?"

"More perhaps than not. Again, we will investigate the east wing tomorrow if we have to break down the doors ourselves."

Watson clicked his horse to movement and they continued forward. "What I do not understand is why he showed his hand that night in the water fountain. Why make a move then."

"Because he recognized you as the one who escorted Lady Pearl back to her Aunt Agnes's in London. He must have realized that you were here to help her and it forced him to move forward with his plans for her demise. As I said earlier, Winston and Daniel are already considered dead by the community. Once Lady Pearl has done away with herself from grief, it will undoubtedly be the conclusion of the local doctor and the inquest as such, and no questions will be asked. At that point, the killer will be able to dispose of Winston and Daniel as was the original intent, and as we have not been able to find them thus far, I am sure he believes no one will ever find them later. It is the perfect plan."

"Yes, but why attack Dorthea? Surely that foregoes the grief stricken widow suicide?"

"Yes, that is true. But I don't think he meant to choke her that night. He meant to draw her to the pool and hold her in the water, drowning her. He saw he was cornered by you rushing from the building and me from the side of the house. He had already drawn her out and she was in his arms. Once he realized we were at hand, his game was up. He made a spur of the moment decision to choke her and once you fired that shot, it startled him into escape. He had to get away so he could try another day."

"I see. Then what has the book of Gray secrets have to do with all of this?"

"I don't know. It may be nothing more than that; a book of secrets. But I do not believe so. What we have learned thus far is that the Grays were not people of wealth. They were pirates; blood thirsty, plundering pirates. They killed each other for the twenty-two chests of gold and jewels. Through the years, there have been strange deaths yet the secret of the book is only passed on to the last surviving heir just before the death of the father. You will note, Watson, that it is always the father who passes this secret to a son. Where are the women in all of this?"

"Strange. Very strange indeed, Holmes."

"Strange enough to be sure, but why."

"Where have you hidden the book, Holmes? Or do you not wish me to know."

"Hit my back."

"I beg your pardon?"

"Hit my back, Watson."

Watson reached over and gave Holmes a solid thump on the back. His fist resounded from a heavy thud. Holmes laughed. "You see, I thought earlier there may be someone always listening. I couldn't leave the book back at the manor. I felt the safest place was with me."

"Very diabolical, Holmes. By the way, where are we going?"

"I have discovered through village gossip that the midwife who delivered Winston is still alive and living in Steverton. We are going there to speak with her. She may be able to shed some light on this whole incident."

"Steverton."

"Yes, it is another twelve miles, and if we wish to ever arrive there, we must step up our pace."

"Steverton it is."

They urged their horses to a canter and the miles of rolling fields and green bordered forests and wetlands sped by. Soon Holmes called out, "Look there's a sign, Steverton to the left, Macsens's Bay to the right. Not too far now."

Steverton was a small but attractive town and they drew up on the main street, called Gold Street, where several people were strolling through the busy shopping area. Holmes asked for directions and with a curt nod, he and Watson set off once more, turning at the corner of Station Road towards Canal Hill. Here they traveled the dusty road of the Steverton Canal. The road was narrow and shaded by the alders that grew thick along the sides. They turned left following a narrow towpath that crossed the planked Mandeley Bridge, and, after a quarter mile, opened upon a small clearing where at last, a thatched cottage roof could be seen ahead.

The small dirt road was narrow and tangled with brambles that had grown wild and spread into the tracks. Around a very sharp turn was the small cottage of Essie Brumholdt. Trees and scrub had worked their way right to the edge of the cottage walls. The steps sloped and the door sagged precariously off the hinges.

"Are you sure anyone actually lives here, Holmes?"

"These were the directions I was given, Watson." Holmes dismounted and tethered the reins to a low hanging branch. Watson followed. They stepped through the knee high grass and brambles and skirted the steps to the door.

"Anything I can do for you gentlemen?" came a graveled voice from behind. Both Holmes and Watson turned to see the shriveled old woman who spoke. Her hair hung in tangled gnarls about her wrinkled and weathered face. She stopped at the stairs, gripping the broken rail, her frail twisted hands struggling to maintain their grasp.

"Allow me," Holmes assisted her to the door. "Are you Mrs. Brumholdt? Mrs. Essie Brumholdt?"

"Thank you good sir, and that I am," she said stepping inside. She held the door. "Well, are you wishing to discuss business or stand out there looking awkward?"

Holmes replied with a curt bow, "Business, thank you."

"I expect you'll be wanting tea or something?" she grumbled reaching for a kettle.

"No, we have come on business only, Mrs. Brumholdt."

"And what would your business be and who are you?"

"My name is Sherlock Holmes and this is my colleague Dr. Watson. We…"

"Holmes, eh? I've heard of you. And you there, Dr. Watson. Some sort of detective? What are you detecting my way?"

"We understand that you were the midwife who was in attendance at the birth of Winston Pearl," Holmes began.

"Oh lordy! What have I done to deserve this upon me now!" Brumholdt threw her hands in the air and cried.

"You have done nothing, Mrs. Brumholdt. We simply wish to ask some questions."

"I cannot speak of that. It has been so long ago, my memory isn't right any more, Mr. Holmes. Sides, there is nothing to say that old man Pearl cannot tell you himself."

"Lord Pearl is dead, Mrs. Brumholdt," Watson said.

"Dead?"

"Yes, he died several years ago."

"Dead and gone?"

"Yes."

"Dead and buried for sure?"

"Yes. Why the skepticism."

"You don't know Lord Pearl. He has a way of staying alive despite all those around him that die. He's the devil you know."

"The devil?" Watson asked.

"He sure is. Him and that old man of Miss Anna's, her father. Taught him all that mumbo jumbo, like they was some god or something that could just take a life if they wanted."

"Hold on!" Watson exclaimed. "I am confused. What has Anna's father to do with James Pearl?"

"Everything! Oh lordy, it's a long story, Mr. Holmes," Essie Brumholdt rose and took up the kettle. Filling it at the sink, she put it on the stove to heat. Reaching for the teapot, she said, "I'd best make us a pot. You'll be here a spell.

"The story goes back far longer than you or me was ever alive, Mr. Holmes. Those Gray people were a really tight clan. They were awful strange what with their secrets and all. But my mum used to talk about that old man, Miss Anna's father, when he was growing up. Him and his father. Strange men. Spent a lot of time in them woods that's there and creeping about down in them caves. He was a strange one. There was a rumor that he did not get along with the old man after a time, can't rightly recall what his name was…."

"Conan?" Watson interjected.

"That may be so, but I am not sure. Anyways, they didn't get along because that boy was very strange. People talked about their animals gone missing and later finding them with their throats slashed. Now mind you, if they were found all eaten and such they could be said to be done in by the wild animals about, but to have their throats cut and just left there dead? Well I'll tell you that was a whole nother story. People started to get afraid, if you know what I mean, Mr. Holmes." Essie Brumholdt rose to pour the hot water into the tea pot. She placed the pot on the table and reached for the cups. "Hope you do not mind no saucers. Just cups."

"Not at all, Mrs. Brumholdt. Please go on," Holmes said.

"As I was saying, strange man that. He took himself a wife and that poor girl only married him because he had money. She was unhappy that girl was. Name of Fannie Derha...Derba.. well something like that from several villages over. Pretty little thing. She had two boys, but one died at birth. The other only lived a year or two and he died too. It wasn't long after that this Fannie was found on the moors with her throat cut. She was nearly naked, Mr. Holmes! A frightful thing that. People got to be real scared and they started whispering that it was that strange Lord Gray."

"Why would they accuse him?"

"Some folks told that they would see him skulking around on The Great Tor, near that there Circle of Stones."

"What is all that about? What does the Circle of Stones stand for and all that?" Watson asked.

"You don't know the meaning of the Stones? Lord you city people don't know much do you?" Essie Brumholdt refilled her cup. "Them stones been put there hundreds of years ago some say by the first of the Gray clan. They came from across the seas, from a strange island, and they set up the stones for their worshipping."

"Hold on, you don't mean worshipping strange gods and....and sacrifices do you?" Watson asked.

Essie Brumholdt slammed her frail fist to the table so hard both Holmes and Watson jumped. "By golly, that's exactly what I mean! What else would them stones be for all set up like that in a circle? That Farley Gray was a strange man indeed and they said he even sacrificed his own father on that stone! People say they could see red blood on it runnin free as you please. That they were killed on that stone, their throats cut and their blood all caught up in some ritual cup and then everyone around the circle would drink that blood and paint it on their faces."

"That's incredulous! Preposterous!"

"You don't believe it do you, but you mark my words, that's what was happening all right. That there Fannie girl was found white as a sheet. There was no blood left in her to be looking like that, I tell you."

"Didn't anybody try to stop it, try to do something about it?" Watson asked.

"How could they. The Grays owned everything and everyone. Most people just tried to stay out of their way. That's why the men of the household had to marry women from other towns and villages. Everyone in Cadwith was too scared to go near them."

"And how does this relate to Winston's father, Mrs. Brumholdt?" Holmes asked.

"Oh once Miss Fannie was found dead, the old man, Farley Gray went and found himself a new wife. Can't recall her name but she only had one child with him and that was Miss Anna. Oh, she was a lovely and lively girl but old Farley Gray was mad. Insane mad. He was mean and mad because that new wife of his never could have any more children and that girl was all he had. And you can know what he did to her, can't you? Yes. She was found dead and half naked at that Circle of Stones. Her throat cut and all her blood gone, too. People sure were scared.

"But the years passed and Anna grew into a beautiful woman and suddenly there was this man come visiting at the manor and the old man got them betrothed, he did. He didn't have any sons, you see, and later there was talk that this man, James Pearl, was one of them there druid priests. He was like Farley Gray, and they were never separated. There was strange goings on in that Circle of Stones again and people refused to walk along the moors anymore or even go into the wood that borders the cliffs. Too many strange happenings and things were dying. You know, dogs, sheep, cattle, the such. You know, Mr. Holmes, I can only talk of this cause that old priest is dead. I'd be too scared to say otherwise."

"You have no fear from that quarter, Mrs. Brumholdt. He is indeed dead." Holmes assured her. "Go on, please."

"Well, where was I....Oh, yes..yes..yes.. That James Pearl man. He marries poor Miss Anna and I'll tell you she did not look too happy about it. Everyone in the village thinks that her father forced her to marry him. Poor girl. She was only seventeen you know. But she did what her father forced her to do and she married that man. I think myself that she was frightened of him. I say that, I do. But they'd only been married for three maybe four months when her father died. Never was a cause determined. Just found dead in his bed one day. So that's how James Hawkins Pearl became lord of Gray Manor. Things changed after that.

"They got much worse. Poor Miss Anna never left the manor house no more. She was not allowed visitors or nothing of the like. I was just taking up my duties as midwife in Cadwith, you know, for the poor folk, when I was called in to Gray Manor to give Miss Anna a check to determine if she was pregnant. He wouldn't have no real medical doctor in the house, no sir, not him. And she was. She was very excited but I could see she was deathly afraid of her husband. Oh, Mr. Holmes. He was a cruel and hateful man and I felt so bad for her."

"Then what happened when the baby was born? I understand from the people in the village that Miss Anna died?" Holmes said.

"Some of that's true and some's not. Here is how that happened. I ought to know cause I was there, witness to it all. It was one of those dreadful stormy nights. Rain pourin down in sheets and lightening screaming across the sky like the devil himself was hurling them down. Those thunder booms were so loud they actually shook the house sometimes. And I knew it was going to be a bad night. It was a bad omen that storm and nobody in Cadwith was stirring.

"But James Pearl sent a carriage for me and no matter what the weather one never said no to James Pearl. I got to the house and poor Miss Anna was having such a poor time. They wase just standing there, around the bed staring at her in her pain and no one bothering to help."

"Who do you mean by everyone?" Holmes asked.

"There was that monster husband of hers, James Pearl and the cook, Lizbeth I think her name was and that old husband of hers, a…a..some Jessop I think. They were just staring at her like I said. So I rushed in and took charge. I ordered them to get fresh clean linens and pots of hot water and bring them to me. They just stood there until James Pearl nodded to them then they went and did it. By that time, all of the hired help at the manor just up and left because they were so afraid. Only ones left were that Jessop and Lizbeth woman.

"But Miss Anna, she was having a poor time of it. The pains were getting closer and I knew the baby was coming real soon. James Pearl stood at the foot of the bed and just stared at her. I don't think that man ever loved her, he was so cruel. But soon I seen a little head come out. Miss Anna she cried, oh, lord how she cried but soon the baby came and he was a beautiful little boy with a scruff of dark hair, looked like a little beanie elf you know? But then Miss Anna starts to push and cry again and lo! There's another little head coming. I handed the first baby to James Pearl but he would not take it so I had to put it on the bed next to Miss Anna. The second baby was slow coming and she was in really bad pain. It was several minutes before his little shoulders popped through and then the rest of his whole little body. Another boy and just as cute as the dickens like the first. But when I turned him over to smack his little bottom, they have to cry and get that birthing out of their mouth and lungs you know, I turned him over and there was this bright red mark on his back. Oh lordy, that's when all hell broke loose, Mr. Holmes."

Watson had been so absorbed in the story he had leaned into the table, his face inches from Essie Brumholdt's. "Hell broke loose! What happened?" he cried.

"That James Pearl starts shouting at the top of his lungs so loud he could be heard nearly to Cadwith. Accusing Miss Anna of sleeping with the devil, the mark of the devil was on that boy, that red spot was the mark of the devil and he shouted at me not to spank his bottom but to let the boy die! I was stunned to shock, Mr. Holmes. I just stood there with the baby sprawled on his belly in my hand and the other in the air ready to come on his little bottom. I couldn't move I was so frightened.

"But Miss Anna she came off the bed nearly and screamed at her husband that he was not the child of the devil unless he thought of himself as such and then Lord Pearl he just got mad all over again. He tried to grab hold

181

of the boy but I pulled away and Miss Anna took hold of that child and he began to cry all on his own. I was scared, Mr. Holmes. I was so scared. I let her take the baby and I backed up into the wall away from that man whose face was as red as fire and screaming like the devil himself.

"Miss Anna grabbed hold of both the babies and pulled them to her breast and refused to let them go. That Lord Pearl was so mad! He told her the devil child must die. He said he would sacrifice him at the Circle of Stones and appease the gods and only the good son will be allowed to live. He beat her, Mr. Holmes. He beat her even as she curled on the bed with those babies hiding at her breast. He beat her til she was bleeding and it was only then that I was able to come forward. I grabbed at him, pulled his arms away from her trying to stop him and he hit me in the face and threw me away from him. But I came back up, I did. I jumped on him and was hitting him on his shoulders and screaming for help, but no one else would come to help. He threw me off again and I fell back hitting my head on the table nearby.

"It was a mess that day I can tell you. Broken furniture all over and covered with blood but he finally gave up and stormed from the room. I managed to get up and go to Miss Anna. She was all bruised and had cuts on her head. She was bleeding really bad down there, you know. Going through all that and just having two babies was too much for her. But she was a fighter, Miss Anna. I cleaned off the babies and I stayed with her in that room just as it was for three days."

"What of Jessop and Elizabeth? Didn't they inquire as to what happened?"

"They were too frightened of James Pearl, Dr. Watson. But I had done with my fear. I stood up to him and he stayed away from that room. I gave orders to that Lizabeth woman for food and water and as frightened as she was, she did bring them. Left everything outside the door. Me and Miss Anna made plans to escape, to run away from Gray Manor but we didn't know how to get out. But we ate and gained our strength and soon she was able to get out of bed and walk about. I could hear James Pearl pacing about the hall outside the door and sometimes the door handle turned like he was trying to get in, but I made sure the door was locked each time. I put a chair against it, too, Mr. Holmes and when there was a full moon coming in the sky I knew, I knew then that it was time to get out.

"It was always on the second night of the full moon that the others had all gone missing and later was found dead. I helped Miss Anna put some things together and we packed up the babies in tight bundles and tied them around us. Miss Anna held the child with the red mark, she had named him Stewart and the little one I carried Cornelius. We crept down the hall and got out of the house and were running through the grounds when that Jessop started shouting. We ran, Mr. Holmes, we ran for our lives and Miss Anna was young and swift but I carried not only the child but the bundle of goods on my back. I was much slower. Jessop was so close behind us and I was so slow. I screamed to Miss Anna to keep running and don't look back. Jessop grabbed me by the hair and pulled me back and that was the end. I struggled to protect the baby and that was all I could do.

"It was in no time that Lord Pearl was upon us. When he saw that I carried the good son, as he called him, he took the baby from me and shouted, "I have him Anna dear! I have my son. Winston is what he shall be called and you will be dead to me. You hear me Anna! You and that devil son are dead!"

"Well, him and that Jessop were so delighted at catching and having the baby they paid me no never mind and I got up and crept away into the darkness of the forest. It took me several days of hiding, but I managed to get to the beach below and that was where I found Miss Anna and Stewart all bundled up in that cave. We stayed there for long months, I went out at night and stole food and clothes from the villagers. I didn't want to but it had to be done you see. We had candles and we went deeper and deeper into the cave so James Pearl would not find us. That's when we found them."

Chapter Twelve

Essie Brumholt rose to pour more water into the teapot.

"Found them? What did you find? The treasure?"

"Treasure? No treasure, Dr. Watson. We found the tunnels. They went every which direction but they was clean and dry. They went all the way to Gray Manor, they did."

"Oh indeed!" exclaimed Holmes.

"Indeed, Mr. Holmes. This one tunnel ended in this marbled room that Miss Anna thought was beneath the Gray Mausoleum but there was no way out of that. Leastwise none that we could find. Besides we was trying to get away from Gray Manor not get back into it. But Miss Anna did not want to leave her other son behind. She called him Cornelius, but I heard the people in the village say Lord Pearl had a new son called Winston, and that his wife died in childbirth and that she was buried real quiet and private like and that was that.

"It took us several weeks but Miss Anna found that one of the passages in the tunnel had a staircase that went right up into the manor house itself! She was overjoyed and even though I tried to get her to come away, she refused. She found passages between the walls and she used a sharp piece of metal to dig out small holes in the walls so she could see inside. She found the nursery, but there was always a nurse there and Miss Anna could not get inside.

"It was several more months before Miss Anna found a latch on the inside of the passage and it opened into a bedroom on the west wing. She would go there and sneak about and watch Winston grow up, watching him learn to crawl and such. Old Jessop didn't guard him as much anymore. We were never found so I figure Lord Pearl thought Winston was safe now from Anna."

"You remained in hiding in those caves for nearly a year?" Watson cried.

"Had to. Was naught we could do else wise. Miss Anna was a long time getting well."

"And all that while Miss Anna would be sneaking into the manor house?" Holmes asked.

"She did. She would sneak through to the east wing at night and into Winston's bedroom. She would sit on his bed and brush the hair from his sleeping face, kiss his cheek and all that. Sometimes he would wake in a half state and she would hush him to sleep, telling him Mummy was there and he would drift back to sleep. She was a determined woman, Mr. Holmes, but one night, it was going on three years and she was sitting in his room when suddenly the door was flung open and there stood James Pearl, red in the face and mad as the devil himself. The door slamming against the wall woke the boy and he jumped from the bed in terror. He started to scream and cry and Lord Pearl rushed to the bed to grab him. Miss Anna ran trying to get away and she was nearly caught. Lord Pearl rushed after her, grabbing at her clothes, tearing them nearly from her back and she fought him off, screaming and kicking at him. He was a cruel one, Mr.

Holmes. Always beating on her but she managed to get out of the dress he had torn from her and she ran into the west wing so quick and got through the secret door and James Pearl couldn't find her. He had the place searched from top to bottom then had all the doors locked shut and he was the only one with a key.

"It was then Miss Anna decided to listen to reason and we took little Stewart from the caves and escaped. We ran at night so we wouldn't get caught. We got as far as Steverton here, found this small cottage for hardly no money at all and here we stayed. We been living off the money that Miss Anna packed in the bundle when we escaped and I been doing odd jobs and some midwifing here. We didn't starve. But we didn't live like Miss Anna should have either. Yet, she never complained.

"Little Stewart grew up and went to school. A smart lad and good looking, Mr. Holmes. We weren't here too many years when Miss Anna decided to leave Steverton. I stayed. I am much too old to be traipsing about the countryside no more. But she took Stewart and I figured they were going to some city to find better opportunities for themselves."

"Have you heard from them at all?" Holmes asked.

"Now that you ask, factly I have. That Little Stewart grew himself into a fine looking young man. He come to visit me oh, maybe six months back. Nice boy, there. He wanted to know about his father, about his family. He was so insistent cause Miss Anna never told him anything. I told him. I told him everything all right. I figured that boy ought to know what a monster his father really was. He seemed right happy to know he had a brother somewhere."

"So you told him of Winston and Gray Manor?"

"I did."

"And what did he say?"

"He said he might just pass that way and introduce himself to his brother. He laughed that rogish laugh and said wouldn't it be a start to meet that old James Pearl face to face and thrust that mark of the devil in his face and there be nothing that old man could do bout it now."

"What did you make of that?"

"I laughed with the boy. It would be nothing that old man didn't deserve after all the hurt he caused the boy and his mother. But after he left, I got to thinking. Maybe….just maybe I ought not to have told him those things. I wrote to Miss Anna and told her I had to see her right away. And she came soon after. I told her what I done and she was upset. Didn't blame me at all though. Said the boy had a right to know. Said she would find him and make things right."

"And you have not heard anything since?"

"Narry a word. I can only pray they are all right."

"I believe they are. Well," Holmes rose, "thank you very much Mrs. Brumholdt. You have been very helpful."

"Thank you, Mrs. Brumholdt. For the tea and all that," Watson shook her hand.

Holmes' glance told Watson 'don't say a word yet' and they went quietly, untethered their horses and started down the road. They returned to Steverton where they stopped to eat. It was late before they were back on the road to Cadwith. Neither Holmes nor Watson brought up the story of Essie Brumholdt. Neither said much during the meal and neither said much on the first five miles of their journey back.

"Look here, Holmes," Watson finally spoke. "What do you make of that Essie Brumholdt?"

"I believe every word she said. She was simply too convincing."

"And this rubbish of human sacrifice?"

"I don't think that's rubbish. It would account for the entries in the book of Gray secrets of how those people and children died. It might also account for why Winston and his father had a falling out all those years ago. Perhaps Lord Pearl attempted to tell Winston of the book and was met with this same type of utter shock and disbelief. That would account for the reason why Winston never mentioned anything of his past to Lady Pearl."

"But if Winston knew of the past history of the Gray ancestors, why would he stay at Gray Manor with his wife and son knowing what his father was?"

"It may be that he did not know the entire story."

"But now we know that the tunnels lead from a bedroom in the west wing down into the caves coming out at the cliffs. Holmes!" Watson cried.

"What is it old man?"

"The button! Don't you see! If Stewart is the man attempting to drive Dorthea insane, than Stewart is the man who kidnapped both Winston and Daniel! The button! The button I found in the cave was recent. It was clean, not covered over by years of dirt or yellowed with age. It was a fresh button. That means that somewhere in those caves, somewhere in those tunnels is Winston and Daniel!"

"It would also mean that Stewart and Anna Pearl have returned to Gray Manor and once more are making use of the cave and those tunnels. Once Winston, Daniel and Dorthea are gone, Stewart stands to inherit the entire Gray Manor!"

"Dorthea! Holmes we should never have left her alone!"

"Let's get on, then. There is no time to lose!" Holmes kicked his horse to run with Watson at his heels. Six miles. There were six more miles between them and Gray Manor. Six more miles between knowing if Dorthea was safe and dreading that she was not. Six more miles and the horses, eager from their casual trotting, caught the urgency in the heel of the boot and shot forward, their necks craned forward, their nostrils flaring, their hooves kicking up rocks and turf leaving mile after mile behind them.

"There!" Holmes shouted. "Not far now, Watson!"

Up ahead in the deepening dusk they saw people running to and fro, hands in the air and the sound of shouting on the wind. The horses galloped across the green lawns of Gray Manor. Merryn was already running towards them as Watson jumped from his horse. "Dr. Watson! Oh Dr. Watson! Help you must help! It's Lady Pearl!"

Watson gripped her by the shoulders as both Conrad and Angus rushed towards them. "I couldn't stop her, sir."Angus cried holding a cloth to his bleeding head. "I couldn't stop her. She came into the stable and demanded that I saddle Magnus. She said that Daniel was there in the dark woods calling to her that he would be waiting there for her. When I refused, she hit me on the head and before I could get up or call for help, she had mounted him bare back and ridden off like the wind."

"Quick ,Watson!" Holmes shouted, still on his horse. "Angus, harness the carriage. We may have need of it. Conrad, into Cadwith and inform everyone that Lady Pearl has gone missing and we need a search party. Bring them to the woods with plenty of lanterns. And fetch Dr. Farley! We begin the search there. Go!" He reined his horse wildly to turn and kicked the mare hard in the belly. She reared up, bringing her hooves down with a heavy thud and surged forward in a hard gallop. Watson mounted quickly and was pushing to keep up with Holmes. The horses were already lathered and breathing heavy but Holmes and Watson pushed them harder. They came to the crest of the high hill where the trail could be seen winding into the darkness of the forest. Holmes drew his horse to a halt and was off before it had. Watson jumped from his mount following quickly behind Holmes.

"There!" Holmes pointed. "The branches have been broken, there are hoof prints here. Damn, Watson. We are going to need lanterns soon."

"Keep moving, I hear something up ahead." Watson pushed forward and there in a small clearing was Magnus his hoof raised. Holmes cautiously approached the horse who backed up skittishly. He reached for the loose rope and gripping the horse tightly, looked at the hoof. "Lost a shoe. There's grass and clumps of brush stuck in his mane. The horse took a fall. Look around Watson. She may be lying hurt nearby."

Holmes tethered the rope to a branch and with Watson scoured the trees and brush nearby but found nothing. "Here!" Holmes called. "A trail leading this way."

"We must hurry, Holmes. The light is fading quickly. Soon we will not be able to find our way."

"No, we must wait for the others. They will have lanterns."

"There's no time, Holmes!" Watson shouted stumbling forward. Holmes grabbed him from behind.

"Stop! Watson you hear me stop, you fool!" he shouted at him. "Do you understand the dangers of scaling the cliffs in the dark? We would do Lady Pearl no good if we ourselves are found dead at the bottom! There are horses approaching now. I can hear them. Wait for just a few minutes."

Watson fell back against the tree looking about frantically. Sunset was quick in the dark woods and already the shadow of Holmes rushing to meet with the riders was nearly invisible.

Angus pulled the carriage to a halt and bolted from the seat. He grabbed the lantern and ran towards Holmes. "Mr. Holmes! Conrad has gone to notify the villagers and Dr. Farley. Gwinn and Merryn are rounding up the tenants and they will be here soon," he gasped.

"Give me the lantern and wait by the carriage. You help Conrad and Dr. Farley organize the searchers. Three to a group with a lantern. Keep away from the edge of the cliffs. We don't want anybody getting injured. Watson and I are going to follow the trail down the cliffs and the cave. Tell the others."

"Right." Angus retraced his steps back stopping to collect Magnus and return to the carriage to wait for the others. Already lanterns could be seen bobbing along the roadway. The tenants were already coming.

Holmes held the lantern to the path. "Watson," he said to him, "let us be off. The others will search the woods, we will search that cave."

"About time! I know just where it is!" Watson quickly followed Holmes. The light was faint but the path was visible and he knew its course. Half way down he halted. "The path veers to the left, Holmes. It leads to the cave where I found the button." They trudged through and found the entrance to the cave. Once inside, Holmes shown the lantern about. There were three tunnels; three possible directions.

"Which way?" Watson asked.

"The most obvious is the wrong one, Watson. It stands to reason that if I were a pirate in 1645 and wishing to hide my treasure I would put in a few false trails. Give me a few minutes."

"But that would be a waste of time."

"Just a few minutes." Holmes bent and inspected the rock beneath their feet. The fine layer of sand blown in on the wind was left untouched going along into the right tunnel. He worked his way towards the center tunnel. "See here. This is the tunnel where you and Mr. Upland entered. Here are the marks of disturbed sand where you reached down to pick up the button." Holmes went to the far left tunnel. "See here, the grains of sand have been greatly disturbed. This is the tunnel we shall take. It was only a minute, Watson."

"I am sorry Holmes. I am very anxious about Dorthea."

"Understandably so. She is in the clutches of a madman and we don't know her situation."

"That is no help, Holmes."

"It is the truth. Come."

Chapter Thirteen

Dorthea had done what Holmes wanted. She kept
to her word. Merryn was with her every minute of the
day, a shadow at her side. Angus had gone to tend the
animals in the barn but Merryn stayed. She stared out her
window, at the maze below and imagined Daniel and the
fun he would have playing there. Fun! Where was her
Daniel now? Held captive in some dark and lonely place.
Crying out to her to help…to save him…yet she could do
neither for she had no way of knowing where he was. And
now? Now she felt a captive herself.

"My Lady?" Merryn interrupted her thoughts. "I will
call Gwinn in for a few minutes if that is all right with
you? I will see to your tea?"

"Yes, of course, Merryn," Dorthea answered
absentmindedly. Gwinn? She could easily give Gwinn
orders to leave her alone. But no, she had given her word.
Discouraged, she went to lie on the bed. Gwinn entered
and seeing her mistress resting, left the room, closing the
door behind her. She sat on the chair outside the room and
waited for Merryn to return.

It was mere minutes that Dorthea lay down when the
voices started once more. "Mamma, Mamma! Where are
you to help me? I am lost in the woods, Mamma. You
must take Magnus and come find me. Find me in the
woods Mamma!" Dorthea jumped from the bed with a

start. That's it! Magnus! Magnus would surely know where Daniel was. Daniel had ridden him through those trees time after time and they were close. Magnus would know!

She drew her door open and Merryn was there with the tea tray. "Where are you going, my Lady?" she cried.

"I must go, Merryn!" she screamed. "Do not try to stop me. I must go and find Daniel! He is calling to me!" She pushed passed the two women and ran down the stairs and out the door, Merryn screaming at her back. She rushed to the stables.

Angus was busy with the horses, having fed them and cleaned the stalls. He was cleaning their hooves, the small metal pick raised in his hand when he heard the sound of feet running into the barn.

"My Lady!" he shouted. "What is it?"

"Quick! Fetch Magnus! I must have him now, Angus. It is extremely important. Daniel needs me!" Dorthea whirled towards the stall where the big black was stabled. She threw open the stall door and seized the lead, pulling the horse forward.

"My Lady! What are you doing? You have given your word to Mr. Holmes. I cannot allow you to do this!" Angus shouted, reaching to take the lead from her hand.

"You must, Angus. I am the lady of the manor. Mind me, not Mr. Holmes. It is important I have Magnus don't you see? He will know where Daniel is. He will know where to find him. Saddle him now!" she screamed.

"I will do no such thing, my Lady. You will go back to the house with Merryn and wait for Mr. Holmes and Dr. Watson. It is what you promised."

"Be damned what I promised, Angus!" Dorthea screamed. "I must find Daniel! He is calling to me, Angus, and I must go. I must go now!"

"I am sorry, my Lady, but I cannot let you go."

"I will go, Angus and I do not need your permission!" Dorthea searched frantically about, reaching for the grain bucket from the floor. Swinging wide, she caught Angus at the side of his head and he slid to the floor, blood flowing from the wound. She dropped the bucket upside down and with a quick jump from its perch, landed squarely on Magnus's back. She pulled the lead rope, jerked his head, kicking him in the belly, urging him forward.

Magnus had been stabled for nearly four months and the kick in his belly was only the small nudge he needed to spur him forward. With a wild toss of his head, flinging his mane into Dorthea's face, he bolted from the stable. The lead flew from her hands and Dorthea bent over the black's neck, gripping handfuls of mane for purchase. He flew through the twisted growth of cedars and onto the front lawn of the manor where Conrad, Merryn and Gwinn were waving their arms and shouting for him to stop.

The horse veered and reared on his hind legs, clumps of turf flew from the thrashing hooves and the echo of his terrified whinny reverberated through the air. His nostrils flared and his eyes rolled big and he reared once more before his hooves hit the ground like thunder. He turned and bolted down the road, heading in the direction of the forest, the forest where Dorthea felt sure Magnus would find Daniel.

Clinging to his mane, Dorthea was nearly thrown when he reared. She tightened her knees on his belly and bent low, her face nearly resting on his neck. Magnus ran like the wind, his hooves thudding on the hard ground, his head stretched forward, muscles rippling beneath her where she rode bareback. The wind tore at her hair, stinging her eyes but she didn't care. Up ahead was the narrow path that Daniel would take Magnus and ride through the woods. She leaned hard left on the black's back and he turned instinctively into the forest. His gait did not falter. Magnus drew long strides along the path and soon they were surrounded by trees and darkness. Branches whipped at her face, tore at her clothes, stinging as they tore through skin.

"Daniel! Daniel I am coming!" she shouted into the darkness when suddenly the horse lurched forward, his leg caught in the undergrowth. He hurled forward, landing heavily on his left shoulder and Dorthea was thrown over his head and into the trees

The horse lay on his side, his belly heaving, his nostrils flaring. His great black head lay still for several moments with eyes rolling in terror before he struggled to rise.

"Easy there, easy now," came a gentle soothing voice and a hand stretched out to grasp the tangled lead. "There you are old boy. Up easy now," the voice urged the horse to stand. Magnus rose unsteadily pushing his front legs out ahead of him. Then with a quick thrust he pushed his back legs and he stood, unsure of what happened, his right leg held off the ground. "Nothing to worry," said the voice, peering at the injured leg. "Loose shoe is all. You'll be right in no time. You just rest yourself, old boy. I'll take care of the lady."

The man felt the pulse still racing in Dorthea's neck. He scooped her into his arms, reached for the lantern and continued down the path. He really did not need the light. He had traversed the path so many times the past six months that he knew every inch, every rock, every hole. He turned and followed the path into the cave, taking the tunnel to the left until he came to a wall. The woman was there waiting, pacing.

"What kept you? Oh God, what has happened? Is she dead?"

"No. Thrown from the horse. She'll be all right. Let's get inside. The others are not far behind." They entered the secret passage and the woman led the way through a large open room, down a narrow hall and pushed open the door. The man lay Dorthea down on the floor and locking the door behind him, left her in complete darkness.

Dorthea lay unconscious for some time. And slowly the pain that assailed every inch of her body told her it was time to wake up. Her brain fought between waking and lapsing into blissful unconsciousness but somewhere in the mist of the pain was a small voice that started as a whisper, Mama, Mama, over and over until it penetrated the pain and darkness. Daniel!

She opened her eyes and the pain was so intense it pierced her eyes and pounded in her head. She waited until the dizziness passed. Her entire body ached and she cried out in pain. Her arm was pinned beneath her and she cried when she tried to bring it forward. She froze and held her breath and her heart beat so loudly she felt sure that it would burst. A noise somewhere in the darkness. She edged backwards until she felt a wall behind her and she could go no further. There it was again. And then a small voice said, "Is there anyone there?"

Dorthea dared not believe! The shock of the voice set every nerve in her body screaming, every cell in her brain crying out in torturous anticipation of another sound. And then it came. "Is there anyone there? Father, I heard something…"

"Daniel?" A choked whisper for her throat was dry, her lips cracked and bleeding, her heart pounding in her throat, preventing the words from coming. Her head screamed Daniel, but the words were lost in the beating of her heart.

"Who's there?" demanded a man's voice.

"Winston?"

"Oh my God! Could it really be?" Winston cried into the darkness.

"Father! Is it really Mama?"

"Daniel?" Dorthea cried once more. "Daniel?" Now on hands and knees she crawled through the darkness towards the voices, her aches and pains forgotten. "Daniel? Winston is it really you?" A hand reached out and touched her face. She grabbed it, drawing it to her cheek. "Oh Winston! It is you!" she scrambled forward and into his arms.

Winston's arms folded her to him and he sobbed quietly and kissed her hair, her cheeks, her nose, her lips. "Dorthea! My darling Dorthea! Why have you come here? What has he done? Are you all right?"

"Mama?" Daniel cried, his little hands touching her shoulder. Dorthea reached to him and drew him into her and Winston, holding tight, laughing, crying, kissing their faces, their hair.

"I knew you were still alive! I just knew it. I knew here, in my heart. It told me all along that you were still alive. I could not…no I would not believe that you were dead. And here you are. I have searched for you for all these months and now that I have found you I will never let you out of my sight again."

"My dear, you should not have searched for us. He will do to you what he has done to us."

"I do not care, Winston. I am with you and Daniel. We are together that is all that matters. And we will be rescued. Remember John Watson? You met him in St. Stephens? He is a good friend, Winston, and he and his friend Sherlock Holmes are searching for us even now as we speak. They will find us."

"Sherlock Holmes? The detective from London? But Dorthea! How did you manage that?"

"John insisted I see him…he is a good friend to him. They will find us, Winston. Just hold me and you shall see. They will find us."

Chapter Fourteen

Holmes lifted the light and stepped forth into the tunnel. Cut from the rock it went for quite some distance. They had gone no more than thirty feet when an explosion rocked the entrance behind them. Masses of rock flew through the air and the blast tossed Watson against the wall, nearly unconscious. Holmes lay face down some distance ahead. The force of the explosion had thrown him forward and half buried him beneath a pile of rubble.

He coughed and tried to move but could not. He tasted blood in his mouth. He opened his eyes. "Watson!" he called but the dust, only beginning to settle, caught in his throat and he gagged on the rawness of it.

Watson awoke to the most dreadful pain he had felt in a long time. He lay flat on his back, his legs twisted and aching intolerably. He tried to move but fell back. The pain in his head was so sharp he grew dizzy. It was the dark once more; the dark and deadly dream that had transpired before. A quiet sinister terror had enveloped his entire being since that first night at Gray Manor and so, here it was at last to claim him. The terror in the darkness of the maze!

"Watson!" the voice called once more. "Watson! For God's sake man answer me!" Holmes shouted.

"Holmes? Is that you old man?" Watson eased himself into a sitting position. His throat was burning from the dust and something warm ran into his eyes. He put his hand to his head…blood. "Holmes! Where the deuce are you?"

"Here, just ahead of you. Are you all right?"

"I…. I think so. You?"

"Yes but I can't move for these bloody rocks holding me down."

"Hang on. I'll make my way over to you." Watson crawled forward and his foot hit metal. "Ah, the lantern." He reached for it and gave it a toss. "Still has some fluid. Would you have a match on you, Holmes?"

"I would Watson but it is difficult to reach as I am buried beneath this mound of rubble," Holmes said.

"Oh my way." He went forward shifting rocks from his path until he touched a hand. "Is that you?"

"Watson! Who the hell else would it be?" Holmes cried. "Work the rocks if you don't mind!"

After several minutes Holmes was able to push through the remaining rubble. He reached in his pocket and found the matches. Watson lit the lamp and they stared about them. "Are you all right, Holmes."

Holmes moved his arms and legs slowly then sat up. "As all right as I will be for today. There is nothing broken."

"It was rather fortuitous that you secured that book to your back. It may have saved you grave injury."

"Yes, it rather was wasn't it?" Holmes cast a look towards Watson and saw for the first time the extent of his injuries. "Good God, man! Are you all right?"

"I don't know. No bones broken but my head aches something fierce."

"It is no wonder. Half the left side of your head has been smashed. Let me have a look. You are bleeding terribly," Holmes said.

"It is a head wound. They bleed more so than anywhere else on the body. It is probably not as bad as it looks, Holmes," Watson managed a weak smile.

"Well, it looks bloody bad to me, old man." Holmes pulled the handkerchief from his pocket and tied it around his head knotting it in the back.

"You are a fairly decent doctor, Holmes," Watson once again smiled weakly.

"I have had a good teacher. Rest a moment. I am going to assess our situation." He took up the lantern and skirting the rubble saw that the tunnel had collapsed on the one end only. The other remained open. "I see we will be unable to return by the route which we began. We can move forward, Watson, if you are able."

"I am able. We must move forward and find Dorthea, Holmes. My injuries are nothing compared to what she may be suffering."

"Come then," Holmes pulled him up, "lean on me, careful here, there's still rubble in the way but it clears just up ahead. It seems that Stewart fellow was anticipating our chase into the cave. Somewhere we must have set off the device. Probably a wire strung across the tunnel and we tripped it causing the explosion. Damn it all, Watson. I should have seen that."

"Awful hard to see in the dark, Holmes. You did your best. Let's just move on shall we?"

Some thirty more feet and the tunnel divided in two. "Now which way do we go?" Watson said.

"Let's go left. We can always come back this way if we need to. How are you managing?"

"Well enough. I think I can manage now. Thank you Holmes."

"Good. Let's have at it then."

They continued with the tunnel to the left for another hundred feet until they were stopped by a solid wall of rock in their path. "Damn!" Holmes cursed. He took the lantern and scoured the wall in front of them. "See here," he pointed. "The wall must have a hidden latch somewhere. There are marks along the floor where it swings open." He ran his hand along the wall and soon found a small opening. He reached inside, his fingers grasped a small trigger and pulled. A door slowly opened, and they both stared into another chamber. A chamber stretching some fifty feet across and in the center were three stone platforms each with a stone coffin on top.

"Holmes! There in the niche! A lantern...ah and it is nearly full!"

"Thank goodness, for ours is nearly empty." Holmes lit the fresh lantern. They walked around the crypt. An octagon shape and to the far left at the back was a set of stairs that went upward. Lying on the stairs was a skeleton.

"A woman, by the folds of the material. Look here, Watson. These must be her bags. They are still in fine shape as is she."

"You are not going to rummage through them, are you?" Watson declared.

"It is the only way we are going to find out whether she is…..ah, here it is. Just what I suspected, the nanny."

"Ruth Charbane? What is she doing down here?"

"By the look of things she was thrown down here by James Pearl."

"Poor woman. Look here, Holmes, claw marks where she tried to claw her way at the door. Apparently this door leads to the mausoleum above us. It must be very well hidden. We did not notice it at all." Watson came back down the stairs. "It is Ruth Charbane then? Poor woman. What else is in that bag?"

"Let's see here. A book of sorts... a diary. There are only a few pages written on. Seems she was attempting to write things down when she was interrupted. Says here, she made a grave mistake in telling the boy that her sister delivered his father. 'I must get out, he has found me out, the good God in heaven help me!' and that appears all she was able to write. No wait, here at the end, 'I have been found out. Lord Pearl is much stronger than they know. He has dragged me here and thrown me down with the dead. He came back the next day and threw in my bags and laughed in my face. Told everyone that I had an argument with him and just up and left. No one will be looking for me, he says. No one. Not even the God I pray to can save me now. He has sealed this tomb and my fate. I am afraid it is the same fate as my sister. I go in peace to be with her for I am sure he has done to her what he has done to me and so many others.'"

"What a horrible end for the poor woman. And her sister?"

"That must be Essie Brumholdt. It was she who delivered Winston and his brother. I am sure that is whom she is speaking of."

"She must have thought her sister met the same fate as herself."

"Yes, and there is nothing more we can do for her, so let's have a look about."

"Holmes!" cried Watson at the coffins. "Tobias Roberts Gray. This one is Jack Easton Gray and the last is Nathaniel Ward Gray. Good grief! These are the coffins of the three original pirates that Hebercomb Hawkins Gray killed for the treasure!"

"They all stole the treasure, Watson," Holmes said coming down from the stairs. "But I don't think their bodies are in there."

"Well most certainly not after all these years, yet their skeletons…"

"No, Hebercomb Hawkins Gray would most certainly not have built a crypt to house the bodies of his betrayers. But, he most certainly would build a crypt to house the stolen chests of gold and jewels, wouldn't you agree?"

"Buried here? In the coffins?"

"Yes, can you manage to help me. I'd like to push the lid back on one of these if nothing else for curiosity sake."

"Of course, let's have a go at it."

They each gripped a corner and pushed. Slowly the lid of the coffin of Nathaniel Ward Gray slid back. Holmes raised his light and the blinding glow of gold and jewels reflected onto the walls of the tomb. Watson caught his breath. "Oh my!" was all he could manage.

"All these years, Watson. Hundreds of years and no one had any clue that the treasure was buried here."

"Old Hebercomb must have used only as much of the treasure as he needed to set himself up here and hid the rest. Imagine, if all three of these coffins are filled with such riches as this!"

"Unbelievable! The Pearl's will be worth in the millions; millions upon millions, an amount unfathomable in today's world."

"Pearl's!" Watson looked aghast. "We have forgotten about Dorthea. These riches mean nothing if we do not rescue her, Holmes."

"Come then. Let's retrace out steps and take the other fork in the tunnel. Are you able?"

"Yes, do let us hurry. We have wasted more time than we should have."

The right fork curved and twisted for more than a hundred yards when once more Holmes and Watson were met by a wall of rock. Holmes felt along the outline of wall and once again found the small hole with the trigger device that swung the door open. The tunnel had now opened into a larger chamber where several lamps were lit along the wall. Holmes moved forward along one wall and Watson skirted the other. A quick nod from Holmes, and Watson silently withdrew his revolver. They advanced into the empty open space.

There was a wooden table with four chairs to one side. Crates and boxes and several of the old chests from *The Gray Lady* were stacked high with pots and pans, some dishes and cutlery and some food. There were several passages leading from the main room, two to the left and one to the right. A rustle of cloth and the approach of voices stopped Watson and Holmes.

They waited and the voices grew closer. "But I am telling you, Stewart. This has got to end. He is your brother after all. It should never have gone this far," the woman cried.

"Mother," the man Stewart replied, "I had no intention of things turning out this way. But the deeper I got into it, the more twisted events became and there was no backing out." They entered into the opened area unaware that the rock wall was open.

Holmes and Watson stepped from the shadows, the revolver pointed at the man and woman. "If you would please put your hands in the air?"

The woman gasped and the man swung around, fear and anger mixed upon his face. "How…"

"Never mind how, Mr. Pearl. Just do as the man says and the both of you put your hands in the air," Holmes stepped beside Watson.

The pair slowly put their hands up. "Tie them, Holmes. I daresay they won't try anything when challenged with the barrel of a gun in their face."

Holmes found several coils of rope. "Sit here," he ordered the man, "and put your arms behind your back." The man sat and Holmes tied his hands together then to the next chair. "Now you," he faced the woman, "sit!" She obeyed, perplexed by the suddenness of their capture.

"But how…we…"

"Yes, we know all about you, Stewart Pearl. And you must be Anna Gray Pearl."

"Enough of this!" Watson shouted thrusting the gun into Stewart's face. "Where are they? Where is Dorthea? Where are Winston and Daniel? You have inflicted atrocities upon this family, your family. A family that has done you no harm! Where are they?" he shouted angrily.

"Stewart tell them!" cried Anna Pearl.

"They are there," Stewart motioned with a nod of his head. "There is a passage and several locked cells. They are there."

"Locked? Where is the key?" demanded Watson.

"It is there, hanging," Anna Pearl indicated the wall behind Stewart. Holmes quickly grabbed the key from the nook and a lantern.

"Stay with these two, Watson. I will get them." Holmes moved quickly down the narrow passage that ran for several feet before the first door was seen. It was empty. A few feet more and he came to the locked door. He keyed and pushed it open. Crouched in the corner was Winston Pearl, his arms about Dorthea with Daniel between them both. Dorthea ran to Holmes throwing herself into his arms, knocking him backwards.

"Oh, Mr. Holmes! You have found us! You have found us!" she cried. She clung to him, crying and laughing both at the same time. "I told you, Winston. I told you Mr. Holmes would come. And where is John?"

"He is holding the captors at bay with a gun. Are you able to walk, Lord Pearl?"

"Yes, I am weak but not severely injured." Holmes put the boy aside and gave his shoulder to Lord Pearl.

"And you must be Daniel?" Holmes asked of the boy.

"I am, sir."

"You look like a strong and sturdy lad. Do you think you can manage the lantern while I assist your father?"

"I can, sir," Daniel Pearl reached for the lantern, his thin skeletal arm looked barely strong enough to support its weight.

"I shall help, too," Dorthea stepped beside Winston "Lean on us, my dear, we will get you out. We will get us all out shan't we, Mr. Holmes?"

"That is why we are here, Lady Pearl." They went slowly back to the large chamber

"John!" Dorthea cried out rushing into Watson's arms. "I knew you and Mr. Holmes would come. I knew it. Oh John! Are you all right? You look horrible! You are covered in blood, your head, it bleeds through the bandaging!"

"I feel horrible, my dear, but I am all right thanks to the medical services of Holmes, although his bedside manner needs some work," Watson hugged her to him. "Here, sit….sit…"

Winston's eyes slowly adjusted to the brightness in the open chamber and came to rest on the woman at the table. "You!" he shouted and pointed to her. "You! You are the witch of my dreams! The witch who would come to my bed and try to snatch me away!"

Quietly she said, "I am no witch, Winston. I am your mother."

"My mother! Be damned that you are my mother! She died at my birth. My father said so. You...you... who do you think you are, you...you...witch!" he screamed.

Slowly, slowly the man whose back was to Winston turned to face him. "She is no witch, brother. She *is* our mother." Stewart Pearl for the first time stared face to face with the blood kin he had been born with. Winston's face turned an ugly gray then completely white and his knees buckled as the shock and horror of looking at himself without a mirror became clear.

"But this cannot be!" he cried.

"Father!" cried Daniel. "He looks exactly like you!"

"What is the meaning of this, Mr. Holmes?" Dorthea cried. She hurried to Winston and eased him into a chair.

"There is water there," Anna Pearl nodded.

Daniel poured water for his father and Holmes said, "I think it's about time there were some explanations, don't you Anna Pearl?" Holmes queried.

"Yes, you are correct," she sighed with resignation. "It has been such a long time, such a long tragic past that I have tried to put it out of my memory. But even as tragic as the events were, there is no erasing it from my mind."

"Go ahead, Mother. Tell them all of it," Stewart said. "Do not hold back. My brother deserves to know the truth about our father!"

"My father was Farley Bartholomew Gray. He was a cruel man not only to me but everyone he was acquainted with. I knew there were things going on, secret things, strange things. Father had a very strict father, one who spoke of the devil, the evil that lurks about drawing people to do bad things. He spoke of the mark of the devil and he pounded his beliefs into my father so much so that he began to believe that he was put on the earth to save mankind.

"I was fifteen when I discovered my Father was some sort of priest to a Druid religion of long ago. But it wasn't a true Druid religion. He fell in with a cult, a group of traveling men who called themselves the New Druid religion. Their mission was to rid the world of the evil, to expel the devil from all that was said to be bad. There were sacrifices on the Tor, at the Circle of Stones. At first it was small animals; then larger animals. Their meetings were secret and only those chosen to follow were allowed in.

"When he was younger, my father married a young beautiful girl from another village. She bore him two children. The first, a daughter, died at childbirth, so it was said, but it was also said that she bore the mark of the devil upon her back. The second was a son. The boy, according to my father, was perfect in every sense of the word. But there was a riding accident when the boy was only five and he was killed. My father felt he was being punished by his god because he still had not rid the world of evil. Throughout the years, many children were found dead. They were weak children, children that were slow, children born with a strange mark upon them. He was such a commanding figure in the community that everyone was afraid to say or do anything against him. They simply mourned their loss.

"Then my father married once more. It was my mother and then I was born. Father was already old by then and yet he still instilled fear in everyone about him. My mother was deathly afraid of him and too afraid to try to run away. I grew to know her fear. She died when I was seven. She was found at the Circle of Stones, her blood drained from her body. The rumor was that whenever there was a sacrifice, the priests would gather after the killing and drink the blood of the dead in that way their tainted soul could not return to the living and they, being the chosen priests to rid the world of evil, were immune to the evil that may have been in their tainted blood.

"I know you do not believe me. I can see by the looks upon your faces, but I swear with all my heart that it is true!" she cried looking at the white faces of shock around her.

"I was nearly sixteen when James Pearl arrived at Gray Manor. I did not know it but he was a priest of my father's religion in another region of Cornwall and came to Gray Manor at my father's summons. My father had no son to inherit. The manor stood to be mine but I could not inherit as a single woman. I had to be married and in that way, the entire estate would be passed to my husband, not to me. My father made arrangements that as soon as I was of age, I would marry James Pearl. I was seventeen the day my father had us married.

"I grew to fear James with all my heart and soul. He was more cruel than even my father, a cruelness I thought could never be possible in a human being, and through all my growing up years I could have doubted that there would be no one left on the earth to be as cruel as Farley Gray. But there he was. He was my husband and it was only a matter of months after our marriage that my father died. It was also then that I found myself to be with child," Anna Pearl coughed.

"Untie her, Mr. Holmes," Winston said. "Daniel, fetch her some water."

"Yes, Father," Daniel rushed forward.

"Untie her?" shouted Watson. "She has nearly killed you all and you wish to untie her?"

Winston raised his eyes to Watson, a look of sadness and loss. "Yes, for she is after all, my mother."

"But…" Watson began.

"And Stewart," Winston said.

"As you wish," Holmes undid the knots and Anna Pearl drank deeply of the fresh water Daniel brought her.

"Thank you, Daniel. It is much more than I deserve from you. From any of you," she said to them.

"Continue, Mother," Stewart shifted in his ropes for Holmes had not yet untied him. "They must know all of it. Leave nothing out. It has been you who has suffered all these long years. Suffered at the hands of that madman you called a husband."

"Yes, it was, Stewart, but these good people had nothing to do with that, did they?" she said to him. She looked to the others and continued. "I was going to have a child and I prayed to the good Lord above that it would not be a son. It was always the son, you see, that was to carry on the legacy of the Gray's. I was not told much of the past, of Father's ancestors but I believe he did tell James everything for once Father had died, James changed. He became even more fierce and cruel. He openly sacrificed at the Circle of Stones and he somehow always had money, a lot of money.

"When my time came, the midwife was sent for. She had grown to be my close friend and in my distress during those months I had confided in her much more than I should have. I put her in as much danger as I myself was in. But she came when she was called. Came to my bed that evening as I labored with the birthing pains. She was Essie Brumholdt. She was a foreigner to our parts but she was a good midwife and in the end, a true and loyal friend.

"She came that night and after much pain, you were born, Winston. I had named you Cornelius but I found later that your father named you Winston. It is a good name. It suits you. But you were born first. You were perfect and James was holding you high to his god and asking their blessings of this perfect boy when I had the pains again and then there was another baby, another boy. My Stewart," Anna Pearl looked fondly at the man still tied to the chair.

"James set you down on the bed and became worried when Essie could not get you to cry. Babies have to cry when born to expel the fluid caught in their throat, you see. Essie turned you over to thump your behind and that's when James truly went insane. He saw the red mark on the baby's back and began to shout and scream that he was a spawn of the devil, that I was some sort of witch to be in league with the devil to have born one perfect child and one devil child and that the child must be sacrificed at the Circle of Stones. He tried to take Stewart and that's when he began to cry. Poor Essie! She struggled with James, taking the baby from him and thrusting him in my arms. I grabbed hold of the both of you and pulled you close. James was so angry he slapped and beat on poor Essie until she was on the floor crying and bleeding. Then he turned on me.

"He fought to grab the boys from me but I held fast. He beat me until I could not see and Essie once more jumped from the floor and tried to make him stop. He hit her so hard she tumbled across the room, knocking the table and everything to the floor. I think it was the crash that stopped him. It was the only noise that was louder than him. He was gasping for breath, his fists ready to hit once more. His eyes were wild and he had the look of the insane. I was so afraid; afraid for my boys and for Essie. But he turned to me then, calm as calm could be. He said in three days would be the second night of the full moon and the baby would be sacrificed just as all the others who had carried the devil's mark had been.

"Essie and I packed up as much as we could, I took all my jewels and the money that was in my room. I carried Stewart and Essie carried you Winston. We crept out of the house late at night and were nearly out to the road when we heard the horse coming swiftly upon us. I screamed and ran into the wood. I thought Essie was right behind me but she insisted on carrying the heavier load and she was far behind. He got hold of her, tearing her clothes and knocking her to the ground. He grabbed the baby, stripped it to make sure it was the perfect son, then he shouted to me that he had won. Essie managed to escape from him. But it seemed that once he had you, he didn't care about us.

"We made it into the caves here through the tunnels. Found this room and found the stairs that lead up into the west wing of the house. We stayed here for several years, Essie stealing from the farmers and I went into the house, found the secret passages between the walls. I managed to steal some clothes, some food. But most important, I found your room, Winston. I would come in at night and sit with you, hold your hand, hum softly to you. There's a secret door that opens up into the blue bedroom and that's how I was getting in and out of the house.

"One night, when you were about three, I was in your room and suddenly the door was thrown open and James stood there. He filled the doorway with his black cape, his face red and fierce looking like the devil himself. I screamed when he rushed around the side of the bed and I threw myself over the top, over the top of you and tried to escape through the door. He caught my hair and pulled me back. He was so angry he was shouting he would kill me, that I was the she devil, that I would die this time and Winston would then be safe.

"You, Winston were on the bed screaming in terror, your shrieks were so piercing they even stopped James for one moment. His grip slackened on my hair for that moment but it was enough time for me to manage to scramble back to my feet and run. And run I did. I ran as fast as my legs would go, as long as my lungs drew breath and I escaped behind the door in the blue bedroom. I heard him coming. He was throwing things out of his way, smashing glass, breaking chairs, I could hear it all through the door. But he did not know of the secret chambers and he grew even more insane with each moment that he could not find me. I hurried back through the tunnels and as quickly as we could Essie and I once more packed up what little we had and left. We traveled by night. We got as far as Steverton and found that small house and moved in there. After a while Essie wanted to stay but I did not. Now that James knew we were alive, he would stop at nothing to find us. And this time I knew he would kill us.

"I took Stewart and we left. We traveled to Harlech in Wales. We settled there. It was difficult but we managed. I found out that Stewart had gone to visit Aunt Essie, as he would call her, and that she told him of that night. When I received his letter telling me what his plans were, I traveled to Steverton and spoke with her. I know she meant well, Winston, but she did not know how adverse the information of our past would affect Stewart.

"I followed him to London where he had followed Dorthea. I wanted to be sure she was safe and unharmed. I...I swear...I swear to all of you that I did not know that you and Daniel were being held captive here until I returned here. I tried to tell him to let you go, that you had nothing to do with the sins of your father, but he was so hurt, so angry, so convinced that he was doing the right thing...."

"Oh, Winston!" Anna Pearl cried. "He did not mean to do those things! He was only trying to make a better life for me, for us. Please, please do not send him to the gallows for surely that is where he will go!"

Silence filled the room for some moments before Stewart Pearl rose from his chair. Both Holmes and Watson hastened to prevent him, but he went around the table then came to stop before his brother Winston. He dropped to his knees and put his head to his chest. "I will beg of you dear brother, to show no mercy to me as I had not done so for you. But if it is in your heart to show mercy for my mother, for *our* mother, then let that be so. She has done no wrong here but be wronged indeed, by the foul manner and deeds of our very own father. I understand now that when Aunt Essie related to me the incidents of that night I felt such a hateful anger as I had never known. I directed that anger towards you and your family, a brother and his family I had never known nor attempted to know. I was mistaken in my anger. It was directed at my father, our father, and instead I hurt the one true family I could have known. For that I am sorry. As for me, I deserve whatever comes to me. It was my doing and mine alone that has brought us to this stage."

Winston turned to Dorthea, their hands entwined, and in her eyes he saw what he already knew. What he had already decided.

Holmes saw the exchange and said, "Perhaps we should let the law decide upon this matter?"

"There is no matter to decide or discuss, Mr. Holmes, surely you can understand that. This whole incident was a misunderstanding, begot and perpetrated by my father more than thirty years ago. It is he and all of his ancestors that have brought us to this stage with their deceit, trickery and hatred. I shall have no more of it. My brother and my mother will be released."

"Oh, Winston!" cried Anna Pearl. She fell to her knees and hugged him about his legs.

"Mother! Get up! You have been threatened and abused and have lived your life in repentance for the sins that others have committed. That shall be no more. You and Stewart will join Dorthea and Daniel and I, and all together, all of us will live our lives at Gray Manor. We shall be equals in all things, for that is how it should have been from the beginning and would have been but for the insanity of our father."

Stewart said, "How can you be forgiving after all I have done both to you and your son?"

"My dear brother. In my heart of hearts I always felt there was something amiss with my life, with my past, yet I could not lay a finger on it. I understand fully now about the past, about the nightmares. I would dream over and over again of that night, that night when our mother was at my bedside when Father came in. I can still recall the screaming, the struggling, the cries of the devil for it was Father who told me she was the she-witch that spawned devil children. He told me that she was the she-witch that would come in the night into children's bedrooms and snatch them away for the devil to feast on. I was deathly frightened of her for all that he said to me. I grew up terrified of being alone and he preyed on my fear.

"I remember growing up, all those times he would become angry when I did not do as he intended. He would shout devil child, and I never understood. How I could be a devil child when he himself had protected me from the she-witch. And when I returned from university is when it all came to a head. It was one cold and raining night. Father was in the library and sent for me. He began to tell me about the book. About the legacy that now I must carry on.

"The more he spoke of its contents, the more sick I became at the absolute slaughter and horror that had been perpetrated by my family name over the years. I closed my eyes and ears and I did not wish to know of it. We fought that evening like we had never fought before. He was insane, I thought to myself and at that very moment my own father had become the devil himself."

"He told me about the book, Father," Daniel said putting his arm about his father's neck.

"Oh Daniel!" Winston cried hugging the boy close. "You should never have been told of it. You should never know what it contains."

"He didn't tell me what was in it, Father. He only told me where to find it. He said that when I grew up and took control with my rightful ownership of Gray Manor that I should get the book and read it and I would understand what I had to do."

"No, you will never see that book. I would not wish anything so horrible on anyone. When my father insisted that I carry on the legacy, we argued then for I now saw him for what he was. I had no intention to become like my father. To do those horrible things he was speaking of. I packed my things and left that very evening, walking in the rain for he forbade anyone giving me any help, not even a mount for my departure. I left that evening and I never looked back. Not until that day when I received his letter begging my forgiveness, begging me to come back. I should have known he had his own evil intentions. I should have known it was not me he wanted to force his evil claws into but our son. I should have seen the change in him when Daniel was born and I should have taken both Daniel and Dorthea away then and there. Much of this is my fault, you see. I knew what he was. I knew what he was capable of, but what I didn't know was the lengths he would go to to get it.

"You intended no harm, Stewart, and I understand that. Your intent was for the money, and believe me, my brother, there is plenty to be shared. If you are willing to forget the past, so am I. And I believe I can say in all truth and honesty, Dorthea and Daniel will feel the same."

"Oh yes," cried Dorthea. "We have finally come to the end of the darkness and nightmares that have haunted Gray Manor. It is time to move on."

"But how shall we explain this away to the police? To the village?" Stewart asked.

"We will tell them the truth. Even if it means the truth of our father and that of our grandfather. They have a right to know. They will know that we hold no ill will and that I wish not to pursue any action. They will understand."

"Yes they will. They are a good people, Stewart. They were thus even when I grew up here," Anna Pearl said.

"And as far as moving on," Holmes said, "Perhaps it is time we get out of here. Everyone is in need of medical assistance." Holmes bent to until the ropes binding Stewart.

"Right," Stewart rose. "If you will follow me, I will lead us through into the west wing."

"I think you had better let me lead the way," Holmes said. "There is one more part of the past you should know. Follow me. Bring the lanterns, it is dark."

Holmes retraced his steps back to the crypt beneath the Gray Mausoleum. With Stewart's help, they were able to push back the lid on the remaining two coffins, that of Jack Easton Gray and Tobias Roberts Gray. All three were filled with the plundered gold and jewels of the crew of Hebercomb Hawkins Gray.

"Watson and I found the book in the tomb of Anna Gray, up above us. It is a book with many evils inside, but I think it would be wrong to destroy it, Lord Pearl. The book is your ancestry from the beginning of Cadwith when Hebercomb Hawkins Gray arrived here with this pirate's plunder. There was never a mention by him of the senseless murdering of animals or people or the affliction of the devil or the sacrifices at the Circle of Stones as spoken of by your grandfather. All of that was his doing, his evil and insane mind that brought those ills to Cadwith. Of your past, you have nothing to be ashamed of."

"But our father? Our grandfather? Surely there must be an accounting there," Winston spoke.

"An accounting, perhaps. Shame, no. A man chooses which path he is going to follow. You chose the path of your mother, that of goodness and kindness. Those men chose their own path and it led them not closer to God, but to the evil one they were trying to rid the world of. Let it be that. Let it be their legacy, not yours," Holmes said.

"You are correct, Mr. Holmes," Dorthea said. "We will make amends. We have enough riches here that we really don't need to keep the people of Cadwith owing us, do we Winston? Do we Stewart?"

"No," Stewart said.

"No," Winston agreed. "If it is agreement with all here, I propose that we settle our accounts with these people, give them the land they are working and all those in Cadwith will be free citizens, just as we are."

"Now," said Watson, "It is time to return to the manor. There is much healing to be done."

Chapter Fifteen

Several months had passed when Watson received his invitation. The payment from Winston and Dorthea Pearl arrived by post several weeks after Holmes and Watson had returned to 221B Baker Street and was more than generous. Holmes was satisfied with the outcome. Watson was relieved that not only Dorthea was safe but that Winston and Daniel were also.

"So you intend to pay them a visit?" Holmes asked.

"Yes, I have booked passage for this afternoon. I shan't be gone more than a few days. I never really did thank you, Holmes for everything you have done."

"No need, Watson. The payment from the Pearls' was much more than we deserved and so much more than we should have kept, but you know how the rich are. One cannot give the money back, can one."

"No, that would have been rude and insulting. And it seems everything has worked out."

"Yes, the outcome of the inquest. It was a stroke of luck for Stewart when he told his story of finding the vagrant already dead and that was when the kidnapping idea came to him. It only made him guilty of kidnapping, a charge Lord and Lady Pearl refused to press."

"That may prove beneficial in the long of it, Holmes. After all, Winston and Dorthea are kind and generous people. It would have gone against every belief they held had they pressed charges against their own family."

"Yes. There are times when keeping to your own morality and principles outweighs that of justice."

"But don't you feel justice has been served? After all the brutality and horror Stewart and Lady Anna went through? Don't you feel it was about time they had a second chance?"

"I do, Watson. In this case, I truly do."

"And so do the Pearls. Dorthea's letters are quite happy letters. Daniel is really taken with his Uncle Stewart and they have begun renovations on the west wing. The secret tunnels will be sealed off as was agreed by all concerned. Lady Anna Pearl will be staying with them. I wish to make one last visit."

"It's the boy's birthday?"

"Yes, the reason for my trip. Ah, best be off. The train is leaving on time today, I hope." Watson picked up his travel case. "Be back soon, Holmes."

"Goodbye Watson. Give my best to the Pearl's will you?"

"I will. Goodbye Holmes."

"Lady Pearl," Anne entered the parlor her cheeks flushed. "Look who has come to visit!"

"John!" Dorthea hurried across the room and hugged Watson, who blushed with her ardent kiss upon his cheek. "Oh, how good it is of you to come! Come in, please come in and sit. We were just about to take tea. You know everyone of course, and this is Aunt Essie Blumholdt. We insisted she come to stay with us. Family, you know."

"How do you do, Mrs. Blumholdt," Watson nodded to her.

"I am well, Dr. Watson. I will only say one word to you and Mr. Holmes. Thank you."

"Your welcome."

"Mama," Daniel came running into the room, "Uncle Stewart has…..Uncle John!" he ran to Watson and threw his arms about his waist. "Uncle Stewart! Uncle Stewart!" he cried. "Hurry, come see who is here. It's Uncle John! Oh Uncle John, you should see what Uncle Stewart has teached….taught me. He is marvelous at carving and sculpting and we are going to sculpt new stone statues for the garden! Isn't that right Uncle Stewart?"

"The boy has not stopped since our return," Winston Pearl laughed.

"I can hardly wait to see them. But I cannot stay long. I have only come for one reason and one reason only."

"Oh, there isn't any trouble is there?" Daniel asked.

"No trouble at all my dear boy. But I remembered this week is your birthday and I remembered there was something that your mother and I spoke of while on our quest to find you."

"Oh, John," Dorthea laughed. "You didn't?"

"Afraid so, Dorthea. Come Daniel. I know it is a late gift, but it is given with the same love today as it would have been yesterday." Watson took Daniel's hand and led him from the parlor. Everyone rose and followed.

"But where are we going, Uncle John?" Daniel looked up, his eyes huge with questions.

"Your gift was too big for me to carry in so it has been left outside. Here we are. Happy birthday, Daniel."

"A ladies hat box? What am I to do with a ladies hat box, Uncle John? I do…..oh! The box moved!" Daniel jumped back and everyone laughed. "It is some sort of trick, isn't it Uncle John."

"Not in the least. You have to pull the top off. Careful now."

Daniel crept up to the box and the box wiggled once more and Daniel drew back. He cast a frightened look at those behind him. He took a deep breath, resolved to be brave and open the box. He raised his hands and with a quick movement, tore the lid from the box, throwing it to the side. A set of furry paws rose over the edge of the crate followed by a round head of bulging eyes and dripping tongue.

"Uncle John! A puppy! Oh Mama, Mama, may I keep him?" he reached in and pulled out the small golden bundle of hair. The puppy jumped into his arms, knocking him over and immediately began to lick his face. "Oh Mama may I keep him, Stop that, it tickles, you silly dog, it tickles," Daniel rolled back and forth as the puppy jumped about licking his face.

"Of course you may keep him. He's a gift. That's what gifts are for."

"Oh thank you, thank you Uncle John!" Daniel finally caught the puppy and held him tight. The small face looked into his and snuggled into his shoulder. "Oh Mama, I think I will call him Watson. He is smart as well as friendly. Is that all right with you, Uncle John?"

"That's just fine by me," Watson laughed.

"Right! Watson it is." The dog's tongue caught Daniel behind the ear and he fell back laughing once more. "Watson! That tickles!"

www.ingramcontent.com/pod-product-compliance
Lightning Source LLC
Chambersburg PA
CBHW030142180626
46812CB00002B/806